"Spirits Across Globe: A Collection of Ghost Stories from Around the World"

Hauntings, Folklore, and Supernatural Legends from Asia, Europe, Africa, and Beyond"

Table of Contents

1. Introduction: The World of Ghost Stories

- An Overview of Global Ghost Tales
- The Universal Appeal of the Supernatural

2. **Chapter 1: Ghosts of Asia**
    - The Weeping Woman of Japan – Yūrei and Onryō
    - China's Hungry Ghosts
    - The Cursed Fort of Bhangarh in India
    - Cultural Significance of Ghost Stories in Asia

3. **Chapter 2: Ghosts of Europe**
    - United Kingdom – The Tower of London and Haunted Castles
    - France – The Phantom of the Paris Catacombs

- Germany – The Black Forest Spirits
- The Role of Ghosts in European History and Culture

4. **Chapter 3: Ghosts of the Americas**
    - United States – The Bell Witch and Haunted Plantations
    - Mexico – La Llorona, the Weeping Woman
    - Brazil – The Headless Mule and Ghosts of the Amazon
    - Ghost Stories and Colonial History in the Americas

5. **Chapter 4: Ghosts of Africa**

- South Africa – The Uniondale Ghost and Haunted Castles
- Nigeria – Spirits of the River Niger and Ancestor Worship
- Ghana – The Ghosts of Elmina Castle
- Spiritual Traditions and Ghostly Legends in Africa

6. **Chapter 5: Ghosts of Oceania**
    - Australia – The Ghosts of Port Arthur and Quarantine Stations
    - New Zealand – Māori Spirits and the Wairua
    - The Role of Ancestors and Nature in Oceania's Ghost Stories

7. Chapter 6: Ghosts of the Middle East
    - The Jinn of Islamic Tradition
    - The Cursed Treasury of Petra
    - Egypt – The Pharaohs' Curse and the Haunted Tombs
    - The Spiritual and Religious Legacy of Ghosts in the Middle East
8. Chapter 7: Ghosts of Northern Europe
    - Norway – The Draugr and Haunted Fjords
    - Sweden – The Grey Lady of Drottningholm Palace
    - Finland – The Spirits of Abandoned Villages

- Iceland – The Hidden People and Haunted Waterfalls

G. Chapter 8: Ghosts of Eastern Europe and Russia
- Russia – The Ghosts of the Romanovs and Kremlin Apparitions
- Poland – The Wawel Dragon and Haunted Castles
- Hungary – The Cursed Castle of Csejte and the Bloody Countess
- Romania – Transylvania's Vlad the Impaler and Haunted Forests

10. Chapter G: Ghosts of South Asia

- India – The Churail and Haunted Palaces
- Pakistan – The Jinn of Karachi and Restless Spirits
- Bangladesh – The Ghosts of the Sundarbans and Zamindar Mansions
- Sri Lanka – The Haunted Galle Face Hotel and Adam's Peak

11. **Conclusion: The Universal Haunting**
    - How Ghost Stories Reflect Humanity's Fears and Hopes
    - The Enduring Appeal of the Supernatural
12. **Epilogue: Why We Keep Telling Ghost Stories**

- Ghost Stories as Reflections of Cultural Values
- The Connection Between the Living and the Dead

Introduction: Spirits Across the Globe

Ghost stories have been a part of human culture since the dawn of civilization. Whether they serve as warnings, moral tales, or simply as entertainment, the concept of the restless dead has captivated the human imagination for millennia. From shadowy figures lingering in old castles to mournful spirits wailing near rivers, ghosts reflect our deepest fears and fascinations with the afterlife.

This book aims to take you on a journey around the world, exploring how different culture's view ghosts and the supernatural. You will encounter spirits from every corner of the earth—some frightening, some tragic, and others imbued with a sense of mystery and wonder. Despite the differences in geography, language, and belief systems, ghost stories share common themes that resonate with people everywhere: the desire for justice, the anguish of loss, and the need for resolution in both life and death.

Ghosts have always been tied to the cultures from which they arise, embodying local traditions, superstitions, and values. For instance, in Japan, the vengeful *Onryo* reflects a society that deeply reveres ancestors and respects the boundaries between the living and the dead. Meanwhile, in Mexico, the haunting figure of La Llorona mirrors the complex relationship between death, grief, and motherhood. In Europe, grand castles and historic homes are often the setting for spectral tales of betrayal, murder, or unrequited love. In African traditions, ghosts are frequently seen as spiritual beings with the power to guide or curse the living, their presence a reminder of the delicate balance between life, death, and the spiritual realm.

Why Do We Tell Ghost Stories?

Ghost stories are more than just spooky tales to be told around a campfire. They are a window into our collective psyche, a reflection of how we deal with death, memory, and the unknown. In some cultures, ghosts are feared and warded off with rituals and protective symbols. In others, they are honoured and welcomed, their presence seen as a natural continuation of the life cycle. Despite these differences, all ghost stories provide a way for people to process grief, guilt, and the mysteries of what lies beyond death.

At their core, ghost stories often serve as morality tales. In many cultures, ghosts are the restless souls of those who have been wronged, seeking justice or revenge. This is particularly common in stories of women who were betrayed or mistreated during their lives. Ghosts like Japan's Okiku or Scotland's Green Lady remind us of the consequences of cruelty, oppression, and violence, especially towards those who were powerless in life. These spirits demand that we remember them, not as victims, but as forces to be reckoned with in death.

On the other hand, some ghost stories convey a sense of tragic longing. Many ghosts are portrayed as lost souls who are unable to move on from the world of the living, trapped by their own sorrow or unfinished business. These spirits evoke sympathy rather than fear, as they continue to wander in search of closure. La Llorona, Mexico's famous weeping woman, is an example of a ghost whose endless mourning for her drowned children resonates with the universal experience of grief and loss.

The Universal Appeal of Ghost Stories

What makes ghost stories so universally appealing? Perhaps it is because they touch on the most primal of human fears—the fear of death and the unknown. Despite all the advances in science and technology, death remains the great mystery that none of us can truly unravel. Ghost stories allow us to explore that mystery in a safe, controlled way. They give us a glimpse into what might happen after death, offering a range of possibilities from vengeful spirits to peaceful afterlives.

Ghosts also remind us of the power of memory. In many stories, the dead return because they have been forgotten or dishonoured. Their presence forces the living to confront the past, to remember what has been lost. In this sense, ghosts are not just figures of terror; they are symbols of history, memory, and the human need to reconcile with the past. In countries like China, where ancestor worship is a key part of cultural identity, the relationship between the living and the dead is a sacred bond, maintained through rituals and offerings. In such places, forgetting one's ancestors is not only a personal failure, but a breach in the connection between the worlds of the living and the dead.

As you journey through this book, you will notice that ghost stories reflect the places and people they come from. Each culture has its own way of explaining the supernatural, shaped by local beliefs, religious traditions, and historical events. From the bustling streets of

New York City to the remote villages of Africa, from the icy fjords of Scandinavia to the humid rainforests of Brazil, every corner of the world has its share of ghostly tales. The restless dead know no boundaries, and their stories are as diverse and varied as the lands they haunt.

The Power of the Unseen

Ghost stories often thrive in the places where the visible and invisible worlds overlap. Abandoned houses, graveyards, ancient ruins, and fog-covered mountains are common settings for these tales. These places evoke a sense of mystery, where the veil between life and death is thin. In the quiet stillness of an old house or the dark corners of a forest, the imagination runs wild, filling the emptiness with the presence of unseen spirits.

The power of ghost stories lies in this ambiguity. Are ghosts real, or are they figments of our imagination? Do we see what we want to see, or are there forces beyond our understanding at play? These questions have been asked for centuries, and they remain unanswered. The appeal of ghost stories is that they do not give us definitive answers. Instead, they leave us wondering, our minds racing as we contemplate the possibilities of what might lurk in the shadows.

In many ways, ghost stories remind us of our own mortality. They force us to confront the reality of death, something we often prefer to avoid. Yet, in the process, they also offer a strange kind of comfort. Ghosts are evidence that there is something beyond this life. Even if the afterlife is filled with uncertainty, the existence of spirits suggests that death is not the end.

A Journey into the Supernatural

As you embark on this journey through ghost stories from around the world, prepare to be both thrilled and intrigued. Each culture presents a unique perspective on death and the afterlife, shaped by its unique history, beliefs, and customs. Some stories will send shivers down your spine, while others will leave you pondering the deeper mysteries of life and death.

From the haunted castles of Europe to the ancient burial grounds of Africa, from the lost souls of the Americas to the restless spirits of Asia, this collection aims to capture the global fascination with ghosts. It is a journey into the unknown, a voyage into the world of the unseen.

So, dim the lights, settle into your favourite chair, and prepare yourself for an exploration of the world's most haunted places and the spirits that call them home. The stories that follow will take you across continents and cultures, but they all share one thing in common: the enduring presence of ghosts.

Chapter 1:

Ghosts of Asia

The vast continent of Asia, with its myriad cultures, histories, and spiritual traditions, is fertile ground for ghost stories. Each country has its own unique perspective on death and the afterlife, resulting in a rich tapestry of haunted tales. While some spirits seek revenge, others wander the earth in sorrow or even playfully interact with the living. From Japan's vengeful *Onryo* to India's terrifying *Churails*, the ghosts of Asia capture the region's diverse cultural and religious heritage.

Japan –

The Haunted Onryo: Spirits of Vengeance

Japan has a long-standing tradition of ghost stories, many of which revolve around vengeful spirits known as *Onryo*. These spirits, usually women who died unjustly or violently, are said to return to the world of the living to exact revenge on those who wronged them. Japanese culture, with its deep connection to the afterlife through Shinto and Buddhist beliefs, views the boundary between the living and the dead as permeable. Ghosts in Japan are not distant

Specters; they are an active part of life, capable of interacting with and affecting the world.

The Story of Okiku and the Haunted Well

One of the most famous ghost stories in Japan is that of Okiku, a tragic figure whose story has been immortalized in literature, theatre, and film. Her tale takes place during the Edo period, a time of rigid social hierarchies and honour-bound codes of behaviour.

According to legend, Okiku was a servant who worked for a samurai named Aoyama Tessan. She was responsible for maintaining a collection of ten priceless porcelain plates, which her master treasured. One day, Okiku accidentally broke one of the plates. In some versions of the story, Tessan falsely accused her of theft, while in others, the breaking of the plate was the crime itself. Tessan, enraged, demanded that she find the missing plate, and when she could not, he killed her by throwing her into a well.

After her death, Okiku's spirit became restless, haunted by the missing plate and the injustice of her death. Every night, she would rise from the well, counting from one to nine, before breaking into a heart-wrenching wail when she reached the missing tenth plate. The story of Okiku's ghost has been passed down through generations, and it is said that her spirit still haunts the well at Himeji Castle, where visitors claim to hear her counting in the dead of night.

The tale of Okiku is a powerful reflection of the importance of honour and duty in Japanese society. In death, Okiku's spirit is not at peace because she failed in her duty—whether through her own actions or through the false accusations of her master. Her ghost's nightly counting is a tragic reminder of her unfulfilled task and the injustice she suffered.

Cultural Significance of the Onryo

The *Onryo* archetype is central to Japanese ghost lore and has been popularized in modern media through films like *Ringu* (The Ring) and *Ju-On* (The Grudge). In both traditional and contemporary tales, the *Onryo* is a powerful force, often driven by a desire for revenge. These spirits are typically depicted as female because women in traditional Japanese society often held less power and were more likely to be victims of injustice. The *Onryo* embodies the consequences of ignoring or oppressing women, as well as the societal need to respect the dead.

The belief in vengeful spirits is so strong in Japan that it has influenced various aspects of daily life. For example, it is considered bad luck to build homes near gravesites, and many people take care to avoid disturbing the spirits of the dead. Ghost stories are often told during the summer, especially during the *Obon* festival, when it is believed that the spirits of the dead return to visit their living relatives.

China –

Hungry Ghosts and the Festival of the Dead

In China, ghosts play a vital role in the cultural and spiritual landscape. Chinese ghost stories often revolve around the concept of *hungry ghosts*, spirits of the deceased who suffer in the afterlife due to improper burials or lack of offerings from their descendants. These spirits, starved and restless, roam the earth in search of sustenance and acknowledgment.

The Hungry Ghost Festival

The Hungry Ghost Festival, held on the 15th day of the seventh lunar month, is one of the most major events in the Chinese calendar. During this time, it is believed that the gates of the underworld open, allowing hungry ghosts to enter the realm of the living. Families make offerings of food, incense, and joss paper (symbolic money and goods) to appease these spirits, ensuring that they do not cause harm or mischief.

Hungry ghosts are often portrayed as gaunt, skeletal figures with distended bellies and thin necks—representations of their insatiable hunger. They are believed to haunt graveyards, abandoned houses, and other lonely places. If a hungry ghost is not appeased, it may bring misfortune upon the living, causing illness, accidents, or financial difficulties.

The Hungry Ghost Festival serves as a reminder of the importance of honouring one's ancestors. In Chinese culture, the relationship between the living and the dead is sacred. Ancestors are believed to have a continued influence on the lives of their descendants, and failure to honour them properly can lead to dire consequences. The offerings made during the festival are not just for the benefit of hungry ghosts, but also for the souls of deceased family members, ensuring that they are content in the afterlife.

The Legend of Nie Xiaoqian

One of the most famous ghost stories in Chinese literature is the tale of Nie Xiaoqian, a beautiful ghost who appears in the classic collection *Strange Stories from a Chinese Studio* by Pu Songling. Nie Xiaoqian is a tragic figure, a spirit forced to serve a powerful demon who commands her to lure unsuspecting men to their deaths. Despite her ghostly nature, Nie Xiaoqian has a kind heart and falls in love with a young scholar named Ning Caichen.

Their love story is a poignant mix of horror and romance, as Nie Xiaoqian struggles to break free from the demon's control. Eventually, with the help of Ning and a Taoist priest, her soul is freed, and she is allowed to reincarnate. This tale has been retold many times in Chinese opera, film, and literature, and it reflects the theme of redemption and the power of love to transcend even death.

The story of Nie Xiaoqian highlights the complex relationship between the living and the dead in Chinese culture. While ghosts can be terrifying, they are not always malevolent. Some spirits, like Nie Xiaoqian, seek redemption and release from their earthly bonds, and it is up to the living to help them find peace.

India –

The Fearsome Churails and Ghosts of Bhangarh Fort

India is a land of ancient traditions and spiritual beliefs, where the concept of ghosts and spirits is deeply ingrained in the cultural psyche. Indian ghost stories are as varied as the country itself, with different regions and religions contributing to a rich folklore of the supernatural.

The Churail: Vengeful Female Spirits

The *churail* is one of the most feared ghosts in Indian folklore. This spirit is said to be the vengeful soul of a woman who died in childbirth or was wronged by her family. Churails are often described as hideous creatures with backward-facing feet, a detail that sets them apart from other ghosts in Indian lore.

In many stories, churails haunt graveyards, crossroads, and lonely paths, waiting to ensnare men. They are believed to be particularly dangerous to those who mistreated women in life. A churail may appear as a beautiful woman to lure her victim, but once he is in her grasp, she reveals her true, horrifying form and drains his life force.

The churail legend reflects the complex gender dynamics in Indian society. In a culture where women have often been marginalized, the churail represents the consequences of mistreating women. Her vengeance is not just personal; it is symbolic of the broader social justice she seeks to enact on behalf of all wronged women.

Bhangarh Fort: India's Most Haunted Place

Bhangarh Fort, located in Rajasthan, is widely considered to be the most haunted place in India. The fort, now in ruins, was once a thriving city, but it was abandoned under mysterious circumstances. Local legend attributes the city's downfall to a curse placed by a powerful sorcerer.

According to the story, the sorcerer fell in love with the princess of Bhangarh and attempted to use magic to win her affection. However, the princess saw through his deceit and thwarted his plans. In his dying moments, the sorcerer cursed the city, dooming it to destruction. Shortly after, the city was attacked, and its inhabitants were killed, leaving Bhangarh in ruins.

Today, Bhangarh Fort is a popular tourist destination, but it is also infamous for its paranormal activity. Visitors report hearing strange noises, seeing ghostly apparitions, and feeling an overwhelming sense of dread as they wander through the ruins. The Indian government has even placed signs at the entrance of the fort, warning visitors not to enter after sunset.

The haunting of Bhangarh Fort is a potent reminder of the power of curses and the belief in the supernatural in Indian culture. The story of the sorcerer's curse and the city's downfall is a classic example of the theme of hubris and divine retribution, a common motif in Indian ghost lore.

The Cultural Significance of Ghost Stories in Asia

Throughout Asia, ghost stories serve as more than just entertainment; they are a means of preserving cultural values, exploring societal fears, and connecting with the spiritual realm. In Japan, China, and India, ghosts often reflect deeper concerns about honour, justice, and the relationship between the living and the dead.

While these stories may differ in their specifics, they all share a common belief: the dead are never truly gone. Whether they seek revenge, redemption, or simply to be remembered, the spirits of the deceased continue to influence the world of the living. Through festivals, rituals, and storytelling, Asian cultures maintain a deep connection to the spirit world, ensuring that the ghosts of the past are never forgotten.

Chapter 2:
Ghosts of Europe

Europe is a continent steeped in history, with ancient ruins, medieval castles, and centuries-old legends that reflect its turbulent past. Ghost stories from Europe often carry a sense of grandeur and tragedy, interwoven with the continent's historical milestones of war, plague, betrayal, and royalty. Spirits in these tales are tied to specific locations—haunted castles, battlefields, and churches—where they roam as reminders of unresolved suffering and injustice.

This chapter delves into the eerie and supernatural stories from the United Kingdom, France, and Germany. The aim is to explore not only the ghostly tales themselves but also the cultural, historical, and societal influences that have shaped these haunting narratives.

United Kingdom – The Tower of London and Haunted Castles

The United Kingdom has a deep-rooted tradition of ghost stories that span the centuries. Castles, battlefields, and old manors across England, Scotland,

and Wales are said to be haunted by the restless spirits of royalty, warriors, and the innocent victims of political intrigue. These ghost stories are often steeped in historical context, with many tied directly to key events in British history.

The Tower of London: A Prison of Restless Souls

The Tower of London is perhaps the most infamous haunted location in all of Britain. Its imposing stone walls have witnessed numerous executions, imprisonments, and acts of treachery. As a royal palace turned notorious prison, the Tower has been home to some of the most tragic and violent moments in British history, and the ghosts said to haunt it are deeply tied to its dark past.

One of the most well-known Specters of the Tower is Anne Boleyn, the ill-fated second wife of King Henry VIII. Anne's story is one of betrayal and political manoeuvring. Despite initially being favoured by Henry, her failure to produce a male heir led to her dramatic fall from grace. In 1536, she was arrested, accused of treason, adultery, and incest—charges that were fabricated to justify her execution. On May 19, 1536, Anne Boleyn was beheaded on Tower Green, her body unceremoniously buried in the nearby Chapel of St. Peter ad Vincula.

The ghost of Anne Boleyn is said to haunt both the Tower and her childhood home, Hever Castle. At the Tower of London, visitors and guards have reported seeing her headless figure gliding through the corridors, clutching her severed head in her arms. Her spirit is believed to frequent the site of her execution, where her presence is often accompanied by an overwhelming sense of sadness. Witnesses have described feeling a sudden chill in the air or hearing soft footsteps before encountering her apparition.

But Anne Boleyn is not the only spirit said to haunt the Tower. The ghosts of the two young princes, Edward V and his brother Richard, Duke of York, are among the most famous child apparitions in British folklore. These boys were imprisoned in the Tower in 1483 by their uncle, Richard III, who sought to claim the throne for himself. The princes mysteriously disappeared, and it is widely believed that they were murdered to secure Richard's ascension to power.

Over the centuries, their skeletal remains were discovered beneath a staircase in the Tower, further cementing the belief that the boys were killed there. Their spirits have been seen playing in the shadowy corridors, still dressed in the clothes they wore when last seen alive. The story of the princes in the Tower has been passed down through generations, embodying the tragic loss of innocence and the treachery of royal politics.

In addition to Anne Boleyn and the princes, the Tower of London is also haunted by other lesser-known figures, such as Lady Jane Grey, the "Nine Days Queen," who was executed after a brief reign, and Margaret Pole, the Countess of Salisbury, whose botched execution left her spirit restless. The ghost of Thomas Becket, the martyred Archbishop of Canterbury, is also rumoured to haunt the Tower's chapel, seeking justice for his murder in 1170.

The Tower's haunted history provides a glimpse into the darker side of British royalty and the political machinations that often led to tragedy. The spirits that remain are not just figures of fear, but symbols of the unresolved injustices that shaped the course of history.

The Ghosts of Hampton Court Palace

Another famously haunted royal residence is Hampton Court Palace, once the home of King Henry VIII. The palace's long and storied history has made it the setting for numerous ghostly encounters. Perhaps the most famous of its spectral residents is Catherine Howard, Henry VIII's fifth wife, who was executed for adultery in 1542.

Catherine's ghost is said to haunt the "Haunted Gallery" at Hampton Court, where she was dragged screaming to her fate after being arrested. Her desperate pleas for mercy were ignored, and she was beheaded at the

Tower of London. Her restless spirit is believed to relive her last moments, and visitors to the palace have reported hearing her screams echoing through the gallery. Some have even claimed to see her figure running frantically down the corridor, as if attempting to escape her captors.

Another ghost that haunts Hampton Court is that of Sybil Penn, a servant who cared for Henry VIII's children. After her death from smallpox in 1562, Sybil's spirit began appearing throughout the palace, particularly in the area known as "The Lady in Grey's Room." Strange occurrences, such as the sudden sound of spinning wheels (Sybil was known for her spinning), have been reported in the palace's apartments, and her ghost has been seen wandering the hallways.

Hampton Court's ghosts are a reminder of the turbulent lives of those who lived within its walls, from the royal family to the servants who worked tirelessly in their service. The palace's haunted reputation adds to its allure, drawing visitors eager to catch a glimpse of its spectral inhabitants.

Scottish Castles: The Haunting of Edinburgh Castle

Scotland is home to some of the most atmospheric and haunted castles in Europe, with Edinburgh Castle standing as a prime example of a location rich in both history and ghostly activity. Perched on Castle Rock, overlooking the city of Edinburgh, the castle has served as a royal residence, military fortress, and battleground, making it a place ripe for hauntings.

One of the most famous spirits said to inhabit Edinburgh Castle is the ghost of a headless drummer. The origins of the drummer's ghost date back to the 17th century when his drumming was first heard echoing through the castle's chambers during times of impending battle. According to legend, the ghost appears only when the castle is under threat. The headless figure, clad in military garb, has been seen marching through the castle grounds, his drumming warning of danger.

In addition to the drummer, the castle is haunted by numerous other spirits, including prisoners who died within its walls. During the Napoleonic Wars and the American War of Independence, Edinburgh Castle was used to imprison enemy soldiers, many of whom suffered and died in the dungeon-like conditions. Their spirits are said to linger in the vaults and cellars of the castle, where visitors have reported hearing disembodied voices, footsteps, and even the rattling of chains.

The ghost of the Lone Piper is another famous figure associated with the castle. According to local lore, a piper was once sent to explore the tunnels beneath the castle, playing his bagpipes as he went so that his progress could be tracked from above. However, the music abruptly stopped, and the piper was never seen again. To this day, his bagpipes are said to be heard faintly in the castle's underground chambers, a haunting reminder of his mysterious disappearance.

The ghosts of Edinburgh Castle reflect Scotland's bloody history, with battles, executions, and imprisonments leaving their mark on the centuries-old fortress. The castle's connection to the supernatural is deeply ingrained in Scottish folklore, where spirits are seen as guardians of the past, protecting the legacy of those who once called the castle home.

Greyfriars Kirkyard and the Mackenzie Poltergeist

Another notable haunted location in Edinburgh is Greyfriars Kirkyard, a graveyard that dates to the 16th century. The cemetery is the final resting place for many prominent Scots, but it is best known for its association with the "Mackenzie Poltergeist." Sir George Mackenzie, a 17th-century lawyer and judge, earned a fearsome reputation for his persecution of the Covenanters, a group of Scottish Presbyterians who opposed the established Church of Scotland.

Mackenzie's harsh treatment of the Covenanters earned him the nickname "Bluidy Mackenzie." After his death, he was buried in a mausoleum in Greyfriars

Kirkyard, but his spirit is said to be far from at rest. The Mackenzie Poltergeist is infamous for its violent attacks on visitors to the graveyard, many of whom have reported being scratched, pushed, or suddenly overcome by feelings of terror near his tomb.

The poltergeist has become one of the most famous paranormal attractions in Edinburgh, with guided ghost tours leading visitors to the site of Mackenzie's mausoleum. Despite the frightening experiences reported by some, the story of the Mackenzie Poltergeist continues to captivate those who are drawn to the darker side of Scottish history.

France – The Phantom of the Paris Catacombs

Beneath the streets of Paris lies a vast, eerie world that few dare to explore—the Catacombs. Stretching over 200 miles, this labyrinth of tunnels and ossuaries contains the remains of more than six million people, their bones neatly stacked along the walls in macabre displays. The Catacombs were established in the late 18th century, as the city's cemeteries became overcrowded, and it was decided that the bones of the dead would be transferred to the abandoned quarries below the city.

The Paris Catacombs have long been associated with ghost stories and supernatural phenomena. Among the most famous tales is that of the "Phantom of the Catacombs," a spectral figure said to haunt the dark, winding tunnels. According to legend, the Phantom is the restless spirit of a man who became lost in the Catacombs and was never found. His ghost is said to appear to those who venture too far into the tunnels, warning them of the dangers that lie ahead.

The Catacombs are not just a place for the dead; they are also a symbol of the fragility of life. The vastness of the underground necropolis, filled with the bones of millions, creates a powerful sense of mortality, and many who visit report feeling an overwhelming sense of dread and unease. In addition to the Phantom, there have been numerous reports of strange noises, disembodied voices, and ghostly apparitions seen wandering among the bones.

The Catacombs also hold a dark history beyond their role as an ossuary. During World War II, the tunnels were used by the French Resistance as a hideout, while the Nazis also built bunkers in the depths of the Catacombs. Some believe that the spirits of those who died during the war still haunt the tunnels, adding another layer to the site's haunting atmosphere.

Germany – The Black Forest Spirits

Germany's Black Forest is a region shrouded in mystery and legend. The dense woods, mist-covered hills, and remote villages have long inspired tales of supernatural beings and haunted places. The forest's reputation as a place of both beauty and danger has made it the setting for countless ghost stories and fairy tales, many of which reflect the region's rich cultural history.

The White Lady of Freiburg

One of the most famous ghost stories from the Black Forest is that of the "White Lady" of Freiburg. The White Lady is said to be the spirit of a noble person who was betrayed by her husband and died tragically. Dressed in a flowing white gown, her ghost has been seen wandering the halls of the Freiburg Castle, her face marked by sorrow and betrayal.

According to legend, the White Lady appears to those who are on the verge of experiencing a great personal loss or tragedy. Her ghostly figure is often described as radiant but filled with a deep sadness, as if she is forever trapped in a state of mourning. Her story, like many ghost tales from the region, carries a strong moral message about loyalty, trust, and the consequences of betrayal.

The Witch of Ebersbach

Another famous story from the Black Forest is that of the "Witch of Ebersbach," a powerful and malevolent figure said to haunt the forested areas near the village of Ebersbach. According to legend, the Witch was a healer and midwife who was accused of witchcraft during a period of witch hunts in the 16th century. After being wrongfully executed, her spirit returned to seek revenge on those who had betrayed her.

Villagers claim to have seen the ghost of the Witch roaming the forest, particularly on nights when the moon is full. Her appearance is said to bring misfortune, illness, or death to those who cross her path. The story of the Witch of Ebersbach reflects the fear and hysteria surrounding witch hunts in early modern Europe, as well as a reminder of the injustices suffered by those accused of witchcraft.

The Spirits of the Black Forest Inns

In addition to its haunted castles and forests, the Black Forest is home to numerous haunted inns and taverns. One of the most famous is the Zum Roten Bären, located in Freiburg. This inn, which has been in operation for 900 years, is said to be haunted by the spirits of its former owners, as well as guests who met untimely deaths within its walls.

Visitors to the inn have reported hearing unexplained footsteps in the hallways, seeing shadowy figures in the rooms, and feeling sudden drops in temperature. The haunting of the Zum Roten Bären is just one example of how the region's rich history is intertwined with its ghostly lore.

Conclusion of Chapter 2

The ghost stories of Europe reflect the continent's deep and complex history. Whether rooted in royal intrigue, religious persecution, or personal tragedy, these stories offer a glimpse into the fears, hopes, and cultural values of European societies. As you explore the haunted castles of the United Kingdom, the eerie Paris Catacombs, and the dark forests of Germany, you will discover that the spirits of Europe are more than just legends—they are part of the region's living history.

Chapter 3:

Ghosts of the Americas

The Americas, stretching from the Arctic north to the windswept southern tips of Patagonia, are a land rich in cultural diversity and historical complexity. From ancient indigenous beliefs about the afterlife to the ghosts of colonial settlers and tragic figures from more recent history, the Americas offer a wide variety of ghost stories that reflect the continent's turbulent past and spiritual diversity. Each region has its own unique relationship with death and the supernatural, shaped by indigenous traditions, European colonization, African influences, and modern urban life.

This chapter explores some of the most famous and chilling ghost stories from across the Americas, beginning with the haunted houses and restless spirits of the United States, moving to the tragic weeping woman of Mexico, and ending with the ghostly legends of the Amazon and Brazil.

United States – The Bell Witch and Other American Hauntings

The United States has a vast and varied tradition of ghost stories, deeply influenced by its history of colonialism, slavery, war, and the blending of cultures. From haunted plantations in the South to ghostly apparitions in the cities of the Northeast, the spirits of America are often tied to its violent and tragic past. Many of these ghost stories have become cultural landmarks, and some hauntings are so famous that they have inspired books, films, and television shows.

The Bell Witch: America's Most Famous Haunting

The story of the Bell Witch is one of the most well-known and enduring ghost legends in American history. This tale of a malevolent spirit tormenting a Tennessee family has captured the imagination of countless people since it first appeared in the early 19th century. The Bell Witch haunting is not just a ghost story; it is a piece of American folklore that has been passed down through generations.

The haunting began in 1817, when John Bell and his family, who lived in the rural community of Adams, Tennessee, began experiencing strange phenomena in their home. It started with knocking sounds on the walls, but quickly escalated to more terrifying events. The Bell family reported hearing disembodied voices, seeing strange animals on their property, and being physically attacked by an invisible force. The most affected was the family's youngest daughter, Betsy, who was pinched, slapped, and pulled out of bed by the unseen entity.

The spirit soon began to speak, identifying itself as "Kate" and claiming to be the witch of a neighbour with whom the Bells had previously quarrelled. However, the identity of the Bell Witch remains a mystery, with some speculating that it was the vengeful spirit of a Native American disturbed by the Bells' presence on the land. The haunting continued for several years, with visitors to the Bell home—including future President Andrew Jackson—reporting encounters with the entity.

The Bell Witch seemed particularly intent on tormenting John Bell, whom it claimed it would kill. In 1820, John Bell fell seriously ill, and it is said that the Witch's laughter could be heard as he took his last breath. After Bell's death, the haunting subsided, but the legend of the Bell Witch has continued to grow over the years. Today, the Bell Witch Cave, located near the original Bell property, is a popular tourist destination, and many visitors claim to have experienced strange occurrences there.

The Bell Witch story stands out in American folklore not only because of its longevity but also because it features a spirit that actively and physically interacted with the living, making it one of the few ghost stories where the supernatural seems to have had a tangible impact on the world. The Bell Witch legend also touches on themes of guilt, revenge, and the uneasy relationship between settlers and the land they claimed as their own.

Haunted Houses: The Winchester Mystery House

Another famous haunting in the United States is that of the Winchester Mystery House in San Jose, California. This sprawling mansion, with its endless corridors, staircases that lead to nowhere, and doors that open into walls, is said to be haunted by the ghosts of those killed by the Winchester rifle, the gun that "won the West."

The house was built by Sarah Winchester, the widow of William Wirt Winchester, heir to the Winchester Repeating Arms Company. After the death of her husband and infant daughter, Sarah became convinced that she was cursed by the spirits of those who had been killed by her husband's invention. In an attempt to appease these spirits, she began constructing her mansion in 1886, and she continued building until her death in 1922.

Legend has it that Sarah Winchester believed that as long as construction on the house continued, the spirits would leave her in peace. The result was a labyrinthine structure with over 160 rooms, secret passageways, and bizarre architectural features designed to confuse and trap ghosts. Visitors to the Winchester House have reported hearing footsteps, seeing shadowy figures, and feeling cold spots throughout the mansion. Many believe that Sarah herself haunts the home, along with the countless souls who lost their lives to the Winchester rifle.

The Winchester Mystery House is more than just a ghost story—it is a testament to the psychological toll that guilt and grief can take. Sarah Winchester's obsession with the spirits of the dead reflects a deeper anxiety about the consequences of violence, particularly the kind of industrialized violence that shaped America's westward expansion.

Ghosts of the American South: Slavery and the Supernatural

The American South is home to many of the country's most haunted locations, particularly on the old plantations where slavery once thrived. The ghosts of former slaves are said to haunt these places, their spirits restless due to the immense suffering they endured in life.

One of the most famous haunted plantations is Myrtles Plantation in Louisiana, which is said to be one of the most haunted houses in the United States. Built in 1796, the plantation is home to at least twelve different spirits, including that of a former slave named Chloe. According to legend, Chloe was a slave who worked in the house, and after being caught eavesdropping on the family, she was punished by having her ear cut off. In revenge, Chloe baked a poisoned cake that killed two of the family's children. After her crime was discovered, Chloe was hanged by her fellow slaves and thrown into the Mississippi River. Her spirit is said to haunt the plantation, and she is often seen wearing a green turban to hide her missing ear.

In addition to Chloe, visitors to Myrtles Plantation have reported seeing the spirits of the murdered children, hearing ghostly piano music, and witnessing strange lights moving through the house at night. The haunting of Myrtles Plantation reflects the deep scars left by slavery in the South, with the spirits of the enslaved and their oppressors trapped in a cycle of violence and retribution.

The ghosts of the South are not just figures of horror; they are reminders of the region's painful history. Many of the ghost stories from this part of the country reflect the unresolved trauma of slavery, the Civil War, and the racial violence that has shaped its history.

Mexico – La Llorona, the Weeping Woman

One of the most iconic ghost stories in Mexican folklore is that of **La Llorona**, or "The Weeping Woman." This tragic figure is deeply ingrained in Mexican culture and is a symbol of mourning, guilt, and the consequences of loss. The story of La Llorona has been passed down through generations, and while the details of the legend vary, the central theme remains the same: a mother driven to madness by grief, forever searching for her lost children.

The most common version of the story tells of a beautiful woman named Maria who fell in love with a wealthy man. They married and had two children, but as time passed, her husband began to lose interest in her and pay attention to other women. In a fit of jealousy and despair, Maria drowned her children in a river. Realizing what she had done, she was consumed by guilt and threw herself into the same river, where she perished.

However, Maria's soul could not find peace, and she was condemned to wander the earth, searching for her children, and weeping for her lost ones. Her spirit, now known as La Llorona, is said to roam the banks of rivers and lakes, crying out for her children, and luring the living to their doom. Those who hear her mournful wail are warned to stay away, for La Llorona is believed to drag her victims into the water, hoping to replace her lost children.

La Llorona is often depicted as a spectral figure dressed in white, her long black hair flowing as she wanders the night. Her story has taken on many variations across Latin America, but it always serves as a cautionary tale about the dangers of jealousy, rage, and maternal grief. In Mexico, parents often tell their children the story of La Llorona to keep them from wandering near rivers or staying out too late at night.

La Llorona's legend is a powerful reflection of the complex emotions surrounding motherhood, loss, and guilt. Her ghostly figure serves as a reminder of the consequences of uncontrolled emotions and the enduring pain of loss. She is not just a terrifying figure, but a deeply tragic one, forever mourning the children she destroyed in a moment of madness.

In modern Mexico, La Llorona continues to be a pervasive figure in popular culture. Her story has been adapted into films, television shows, and even songs, and her haunting cry is recognized by people across the country. The legend of La Llorona speaks to a universal human experience—grief—and has made her one of the most enduring ghost stories in Latin American culture.

Brazil – *The Headless Mule and Ghosts of the Amazon*

South America is home to a rich tapestry of ghost stories, many of which are tied to indigenous beliefs and the unique natural landscape of the continent. In Brazil, the Amazon rainforest is a place of mystery and wonder, but it is also home to numerous ghost stories and legends that reflect the spiritual beliefs of the region's indigenous peoples, as well as the legacy of Portuguese colonization.

The Headless Mule: A Curse of Betrayal

One of Brazil's most famous supernatural creatures is the **Headless Mule** (*Mula sem Cabeça*), a ghostly figure that roams the countryside, often associated with the sin of betrayal or forbidden love. According to legend, the Headless Mule is the cursed spirit of a woman who had an illicit relationship with a priest, breaking her religious vows. As punishment, she was transformed into a mule without a head, her body set aflame and condemned to gallop across the land every Thursday night, accompanied by the sound of her hooves striking the ground like thunder.

The Headless Mule's appearance is both terrifying and tragic. She is often described as a fiery, headless creature that gallops through the countryside, with flames shooting from her neck where her head should be. Her presence is often signalled by the sound of her hooves pounding the earth and her mournful neighing. The sight of the Headless Mule is said to bring bad luck, and those who encounter her are warned to stay away, lest they be caught in her curse.

The Headless Mule legend is a reflection of Brazil's religious history, particularly the influence of Catholicism and the strict moral codes that were imposed during the colonial period. The story of the cursed woman who becomes the Headless Mule serves as a cautionary tale about the consequences of breaking religious vows, particularly for women. However, it is also a story of sorrow and loss, as the woman is doomed to wander forever, her crime unforgivable.

Ghosts of the Amazon Rainforest

The Amazon rainforest, with its vast, impenetrable canopy and remote villages, is a place where the boundary between the physical world and the spiritual realm is often seen as fluid. The indigenous peoples of the Amazon have long believed in spirits that inhabit the land, the rivers, and the trees. These spirits, known as *encantados*, are thought to be both protectors and tricksters, capable of both aiding and deceiving humans.

One of the most famous supernatural figures in the Amazon is the *Boto*, or the Amazon River dolphin. According to local folklore, the Boto is a shapeshifter who can transform into a handsome man. He is said to come ashore during festivals and seduce young women, who often disappear after encountering him. The Boto is believed to be both a spirit of the river and a symbol of fertility, but his interactions with humans can be dangerous. Women who fall under the Boto's spell are often left heartbroken or pregnant, and the spirit is sometimes blamed for unexplained disappearances in the Amazon's remote villages.

The spirits of the Amazon are deeply tied to the natural world, and many ghost stories from the region emphasize the importance of respecting the land and its creatures. The rainforest is seen as a living entity, and those who harm it or disrespect its spirits are said to suffer consequences, either through illness, misfortune, or encounters with vengeful spirits.

The ghosts of the Amazon reflect the indigenous belief that the world is filled with unseen forces, and that humans are only one part of a much larger spiritual ecosystem. These stories serve as reminders of the fragility of life in the rainforest and the importance of living in harmony with the natural world.

Conclusion of Chapter 3

The ghost stories of the Americas are as diverse as the cultures and histories that shape the continent. From the haunted plantations of the American South to the tragic figure of La Llorona in Mexico, and the eerie spirits of the Amazon rainforest, these tales reflect the unique blend of indigenous, European, and African influences that define the region's spiritual landscape. Ghosts in the Americas are often tied to themes of guilt, betrayal, and the consequences of human actions, serving as both warnings and reminders of the past.

As you explore the ghostly tales of the Americas, you will encounter spirits that are not just figures of fear, but symbols of the unresolved pain and history that continue to shape the continent. Whether seeking revenge, redemption, or peace, the ghosts of the Americas remind us that the dead are never truly gone—they live on in the stories we tell and the places we inhabit.

Chapter 4:

Ghosts of Africa

Africa is a continent that holds some of the world's oldest civilizations, spiritual beliefs, and cultural traditions. Ghost stories from Africa are as diverse as its many nations, each carrying the imprint of the land's history, from ancient tribal lore to colonial struggles and post-colonial transformation. The concept of the supernatural in African cultures is deeply rooted in the connection between the physical and spiritual realms. Spirits of ancestors are often revered, consulted, and honoured, and they can be either protectors or tormentors, depending on how they were treated in life and how their descendants honour them.

In this chapter, we explore some of the most famous ghost stories from various parts of Africa, delving into how spirits influence daily life, as well as how they reflect the cultural values and historical events of the regions they haunt.

South Africa – The Uniondale Ghost and Other Hauntings

South Africa is a country rich in history, from its indigenous peoples to the struggles of colonization, apartheid, and eventual liberation. The country's ghost stories reflect the complexities of its past, with restless spirits tied to tragic love stories, violent deaths, and historical injustices. Some of South Africa's most famous ghosts haunt not only buildings but also open roads, a reminder of the unresolved trauma and memories that linger in the country's collective consciousness.

The Uniondale Ghost: A Tragic Love Story on the Road

One of the most famous ghost stories in South Africa is that of the Uniondale Ghost, a tale of a tragic accident and a restless spirit. The story is cantered around a stretch of road near the small town of Uniondale, located in the semi-desert Karoo region. In 1968, a young woman named Maria Charlotte Roux was killed in a car accident on this road while traveling with her fiancé. Their Volkswagen Beetle crashed during a storm, and Maria died at the scene, while her fiancé survived.

Since then, there have been numerous reports of Maria's ghost appearing to drivers on that same stretch of road. According to witnesses, the ghost is often seen as a young woman dressed in dark clothing, standing by the side of the road, sometimes even attempting to hitch a ride. Those who have stopped to pick her up report that she enters the vehicle, only to mysteriously disappear shortly after the car resumes its journey.

In some versions of the story, the ghost leaves behind a token—such as a scarf or shawl—as a sign of her presence. Others claim to have felt a cold breeze or heard a soft voice speaking in the backseat just before she vanishes. Maria's ghost is believed to be tied to the moment of her death, forever reliving her final journey and seeking to complete the trip she never finished.

The Uniondale Ghost is more than just a local legend; it is a reflection of the emotional scars left by loss and the sense of unfinished business that permeates many ghost stories. Maria's spirit, bound to the road where she met her untimely end, embodies the idea that some souls cannot rest until their stories are resolved.

The Ghosts of Spookhuis

The "Spookhuis" (literally "ghost house") in South Africa is another location famous for paranormal activity. Located in the Western Cape near the town of Kleinmond, Spookhuis is an old Victorian-style mansion that has earned a reputation for being one of the most haunted places in the country.

Built in the 19th century, Spookhuis was originally a hunting lodge, but over the years, it became notorious for strange and unexplained events. Visitors and locals alike have reported hearing eerie footsteps, disembodied voices, and objects moving on their own. Some claim to have seen shadowy figures lurking in the hallways, while others have experienced sudden drops in temperature or the feeling of being watched.

One particularly persistent legend about Spookhuis is that of a woman who was murdered in the house by her lover. Her ghost is said to haunt the property, wandering the rooms in search of peace. Those who have visited the mansion often leave with a sense of unease, as though the house itself holds onto the spirits of the past, refusing to let them go.

Spookhuis reflects the fascination with the unknown that many South Africans share, particularly in rural areas where old buildings and isolated locations carry a sense of mystery. The mansion's haunted reputation has made it a popular destination for ghost hunters and thrill-seekers, yet it remains an unsettling reminder of the fragile boundary between life and death.

The Tokoloshe: A Mischievous Spirit of African Folklore

While many of South Africa's ghost stories are tied to historical events, there are also tales rooted in the ancient beliefs of its indigenous peoples. One of the most famous supernatural beings in South African folklore is the **Tokoloshe**, a small, mischievous creature that is said to cause trouble for humans. Unlike traditional ghosts, the Tokoloshe is a malevolent spirit that can be summoned by a witch or shaman to harm or frighten people.

According to legend, the Tokoloshe is an impish creature with an insatiable thirst for mischief. It can become invisible at will, and it is often blamed for unexplained accidents, illnesses, or deaths. In many traditional Zulu communities, people sleep with their beds raised off the ground, as it is believed that the Tokoloshe cannot reach them if they are high enough.

The Tokoloshe legend reflects the complex relationship between the spiritual and physical worlds in African belief systems. It also speaks to the role of supernatural forces in everyday life, where the line between the seen and the unseen is often blurred. Though the Tokoloshe is feared, it is also respected as part of the larger tapestry of African spiritual tradition.

Nigeria - Spirits of the River Niger and Ancestor Worship

Nigeria is a country with a rich tapestry of cultures, languages, and religions. The Yoruba, Igbo, and Hausa people, among others, each have their own traditions and stories about the supernatural. For many Nigerians, the spirits of the dead remain close to the living, watching over them and sometimes seeking to influence their lives.

Ancestor worship is central to many Nigerian spiritual traditions, particularly among the Yoruba and Igbo peoples. Ancestors are considered guardians of the family and are often consulted in matters of significant importance. However, if an ancestor is displeased or forgotten, they may return to haunt the living, demanding recognition, and respect.

The Spirits of the River Niger

The River Niger is one of Africa's most important waterways, and for many Nigerians, it is also a place of deep spiritual significance. The river is believed to be home to various spirits and deities, known as *water spirits* or *Mammy Water* in the local traditions. These spirits are said to control the flow of the river and influence the lives of those who live along its banks.

One of the most famous water spirits in Nigeria is *Olokun*, the deity of the deep sea in Yoruba cosmology. Olokun is often associated with wealth and prosperity, but also with mystery and danger. Those who offend the spirit of the river may find themselves plagued by misfortune or illness, while those who honor Olokun are believed to be blessed with success and good fortune.

There is also numerous ghost stories associated with the river, particularly concerning those who have drowned in its waters. It is said that the spirits of the drowned sometimes rise from the river, calling out to the living or attempting to pull others into the water. These ghostly figures are often seen as cautionary tales, warning people to respect the power of the river and the spirits that inhabit it.

The Lady Koi Koi Ghost

Another famous Nigerian ghost story is that of **Lady Koi**, a spectral figure known to haunt boarding schools. According to legend, Lady Koi was once a beautiful teacher who had a passion for high-heeled shoes. However, she was cruel to her students, and after her death, her ghost began appearing in schools, especially at night. Her trademark is the sound of her heels clicking ("koi koi") as she walks down the halls.

Students across Nigeria have reported hearing Lady Koi Koi's footsteps late at night, followed by strange noises or unexplained events. In some versions of the story, those who encounter her ghost are cursed or disappear. Lady Koi Koi is often used as a cautionary tale for children, warning them to behave and obey their teachers.

The story of Lady Koi Koi highlights the role that ghost stories play in Nigerian culture, particularly in boarding school settings where students are away from home and more vulnerable to the supernatural. The ghost serves as both a figure of fear and a symbol of the consequences of cruelty, reflecting the moral undertones often found in African folklore.

Ghana – The Ashanti Ancestor Spirits and the Ghosts of Elmina Castle

In Ghana, the Ashanti people have a long tradition of honouring their ancestors, believing that the dead continue to play an active role in the lives of the living. Ancestors are often consulted through divination and are believed to provide protection and guidance. However, they can also become vengeful if they are disrespected or forgotten.

The Ghosts of Elmina Castle

Elmina Castle, located on the coast of Ghana, is one of the most haunting and historically significant sites in Africa. Built by the Portuguese in 1482, the castle became a key part of the transatlantic slave trade, where countless African men, women, and children were imprisoned before being shipped to the Americas. The suffering that occurred within the walls of Elmina Castle has left a deep mark on the land, and it is said that the spirits of the enslaved continue to haunt the site.

Visitors to Elmina Castle often report hearing the cries of the enslaved echoing through the dark dungeons, where prisoners were kept in appalling conditions. Some have claimed to see ghostly figures wandering the castle's corridors, their presence a reminder of the atrocities that took place there. The spirits of Elmina are not just symbols of individual suffering; they represent the collective trauma of the African diaspora and the long-lasting impact of slavery on the continent.

The haunting of Elmina Castle is a powerful example of how places of great historical significance can become imbued with the spirits of those who suffered there. The ghosts of the castle serve as both a warning and a reminder of the horrors of the past, ensuring that the history of the transatlantic slave trade is never forgotten.

The Ashanti Belief in Reincarnation

In Ashanti culture, the belief in reincarnation is strong, and it is thought that the spirits of ancestors can be reborn into new members of the family. This belief is intertwined with the concept of ancestor worship, where the dead are honoured and respected to ensure their favourable return in future generations.

However, the spirits of those who die tragically or unjustly may become restless, wandering the earth as ghosts. These spirits, known as *asamando*, are often feared, as they are believed to bring misfortune to the living if not properly appeased through rituals and offerings. In Ashanti culture, ghost stories serve as moral lessons, reminding the living to honour their ancestors and uphold the values of the community.

Conclusion of Chapter 4

The ghost stories of Africa are deeply connected to the continent's spiritual traditions and historical experiences. Whether it is the restless spirits of Elmina Castle, the mischievous Tokoloshe of South Africa, or the spirits of the River Niger, these tales reflect the close relationship between the living and the dead in African cultures. Ghosts in African folklore are not merely figures of fear; they are part of a larger spiritual framework that emphasizes respect for ancestors, the power of the natural world, and the importance of maintaining balance between the physical and spiritual realms.

As you explore the ghostly tales of Africa, you will encounter spirits that serve as protectors, tormentors, and moral guides. These stories remind us that the dead are never truly gone—they continue to influence the world of the living, demanding recognition, respect, and, sometimes, resolution for the injustices they experienced in life.

Chapter 5:

Ghosts of Oceania

Oceania is a vast and diverse region that spans the islands of the Pacific, including Australia, New Zealand, and numerous smaller island nations. The ghost stories of Oceania are deeply tied to the land and its history, blending the indigenous spiritual traditions that have existed for millennia with the colonial and post-colonial influences that followed European settlement.

The indigenous peoples of Australia and New Zealand, the Aboriginal Australians, and the Māori of New Zealand, have long believed in the power of spirits and the importance of maintaining a balance between the physical and spiritual worlds. These beliefs have shaped many of the ghost stories that persist today, stories of ancestral spirits, guardians of sacred lands, and the restless dead. European settlers brought their own ghostly traditions, leading to a fascinating melding of folklore that continues to evolve.

Australia - The Ghosts of Port Arthur and Other Haunted Places

Australia's ghost stories are tied to its colonial past, particularly the penal colonies established by the British in the late 18th century. As a place where convicts were sent to serve harsh sentences, Australia's early history is filled with tales of suffering, death, and brutality, all of which have left their mark on the land. Many of the country's most famous hauntings are connected to its penal heritage, with old prisons and settlements serving as the sites of some of the most chilling ghost stories in the Southern Hemisphere.

The Ghosts of Port Arthur

Port Arthur, located in Tasmania, is one of Australia's most infamous haunted locations. Once a penal colony, Port Arthur housed some of the British Empire's most hardened convicts. Established in 1830, it was known for its brutal conditions, where prisoners endured hard labour, strict discipline, and isolation.

The harsh treatment, combined with the site's remoteness, created an environment ripe for tragedy and death.

Port Arthur's haunted reputation stems from the numerous stories of apparitions, strange noises, and unexplainable occurrences reported by visitors and staff alike. One of the most famous ghostly residents is the spirit of a young boy named James Lynch. Lynch was sentenced to Port Arthur as a teenager for stealing and died in mysterious circumstances while imprisoned. Visitors to the old cells where Lynch was held have reported feeling an overwhelming sense of dread, hearing whispers, and even seeing the ghostly figure of a young boy in the shadows.

Another well-known spirit is that of Reverend George Eastman, a chaplain who worked at Port Arthur during its time as a penal colony. Eastman was known for his efforts to reform the prisoners, but he became deeply troubled by the conditions at the prison and was later found dead under mysterious circumstances. His ghost is said to wander the chapel, his presence felt by those who hear soft prayers or see a shadowy figure near the altar.

Port Arthur also housed an asylum for mentally ill prisoners, many of whom endured inhumane treatment. The asylum is now one of the most haunted areas of the site, with visitors reporting strange sounds, flickering lights, and the feeling of being watched. Some claim to have seen figures in old prison uniforms, while others have experienced the sensation of being touched or pushed by invisible hands.

The spirits of Port Arthur are a stark reminder of the suffering endured by those who were sent to the penal colony. The harsh conditions, isolation, and often untimely deaths created an atmosphere that still lingers, as if the pain of the past has seeped into the very walls of the settlement.

The Ghost of the Quarantine Station

Another famously haunted site in Australia is the **Quarantine Station** at North Head in Sydney. Built in the 1830s, the Quarantine Station was used to isolate immigrants who were suspected of carrying contagious diseases such as smallpox, cholera, and the plague. Many of those who were sent to the station never left, succumbing to illness, and dying far from their families and homes.

The Quarantine Station's history of death and suffering has given rise to numerous ghost stories, with reports of paranormal activity dating back more than a century. Visitors to the site have reported hearing ghostly voices, seeing figures in old-fashioned clothing, and feeling unexplained cold spots in certain areas of the station. The most active areas include the hospital, the morgue, and the shower block, where many new arrivals were disinfected upon their arrival—often in brutal and humiliating ways.

One of the most frequently sighted spirits is that of a nurse who worked at the station during a deadly outbreak. Known as "Matron," her ghost is said to appear near the old hospital, where she cared for the sick and dying. She is often described as a comforting presence, but others have reported feeling a heavy sadness in the areas where she is seen, as though she is still burdened by the memory of those she could not save.

The Quarantine Station's haunted past reflects Australia's colonial history, where isolation, disease, and death were constant companions for those arriving on the continent. The spirits that are said to haunt the station serve as reminders of the fear and loss that defined the lives of many immigrants who sought a new beginning in a land that was often unforgiving.

The Ghosts of Monte Cristo Homestead

Monte Cristo Homestead in Junee, New South Wales, is considered one of the most haunted houses in Australia. Built in 1884 by Christopher William Crawley, a wealthy farmer, the house has been the site of numerous tragic events, including violent deaths, accidents, and suicides, all of which are said to have contributed to its haunted reputation.

One of the most infamous stories associated with Monte Cristo involves the spirit of Mrs. Crawley, the matriarch of the family. After the death of her husband, Mrs. Crawley became reclusive, rarely leaving the house. She died in the home in 1933, and her ghost is said to still haunt the mansion, with reports of her presence often accompanied by the scent of lavender, her favourite perfume.

Other spirits that haunt Monte Cristo include that of a young housekeeper who fell to her death from the balcony, a stable hand who was burned alive in the stables, and a mentally ill man who was chained up by his father and left to die in one of the rooms. Visitors to the house have reported seeing shadowy figures, hearing unexplained noises, and feeling sudden, intense cold in certain areas of the mansion.

The tragic history of Monte Cristo has turned the homestead into a magnet for ghost hunters and thrill-seekers. The lingering presence of the spirits that are said to inhabit the house speaks to the unresolved pain and trauma that remain within its walls, making it one of the most notorious haunted locations in the country.

New Zealand – Māori Spirits and the Wairua

New Zealand's ghost stories are deeply influenced by Māori spiritual beliefs, which emphasize the connection between the living and the dead, and the presence of *wairua* (spirits) in the natural world. Māori believe that the spirits of the dead remain close to the living, watching over their descendants and interacting with the world around them. These spirits can be either benevolent or malevolent, depending on how they were treated in life and in death.

The Spirits of Lake Tarawera

One of the most famous ghost stories in New Zealand is that of **Lake Tarawera**, a site of great spiritual significance to the Māori people. In 1886, the nearby Mount Tarawera erupted, destroying villages, and killing over 150 people. The eruption also buried the famous Pink and White Terraces, natural silica formations that were once considered a wonder of the world.

Before the eruption, there were reports of strange sightings on the lake. Several Māori elders claimed to have seen a ghostly canoe filled with wairua paddling across the water. The canoe was described as ancient, with its paddlers wearing traditional Māori garments not seen for many generations. The sighting was interpreted as a warning of impending disaster, and many believe that the appearance of the ghostly canoe foretold the eruption of Mount Tarawera.

To this day, Lake Tarawera is considered a place where the spiritual and physical worlds intersect. Visitors to the area have reported hearing eerie sounds coming from the lake, and some claim to have seen the ghostly canoe themselves. The spirits of those who died in the eruption are believed to still haunt the region, their presence a reminder of the catastrophic event that changed the landscape forever.

The Spirits of Māori Warriors

Māori culture places great emphasis on the honouring of ancestors, particularly those who died in battle. The spirits of Māori warriors, known as *tupuna*, are believed to protect their descendants and the lands they once fought for. However, if a warrior's remains are disturbed, or if their descendants fail to honour them properly, their spirit may become restless, seeking revenge or retribution.

One of the most famous stories of Māori warrior spirits comes from the **Wairau Bar**, an ancient burial ground near Blenheim on New Zealand's South Island. In the 1940s, European settlers disturbed the burial site while constructing a road, leading to reports of strange occurrences in the area. People claimed to have seen the ghosts of Māori warriors, dressed in traditional garb, and carrying weapons, appearing near the construction site. Machinery malfunctioned, workers reported feeling an overwhelming sense of dread, and some even claimed to have been physically attacked by unseen forces.

The disturbance of sacred Māori sites is a sensitive issue in New Zealand, and the story of the Wairau Bar is a powerful reminder of the importance of respecting the land and the spirits that inhabit it. The spirits of Māori warriors are not just figures of folklore; they are seen as active protectors of the land and its people, ensuring that the traditions of the past are upheld.

The Ghosts of Larnach Castle

New Zealand's only castle, **Larnach Castle**, located in Dunedin, is a site of historical significance and is also said to be haunted by the ghosts of its past inhabitants. The castle was built in the late 19th century by William Larnach, a wealthy politician and businessman. However, the Larnach family was plagued by tragedy, including the suicide of William Larnach himself, who took his own life in 1898 after a series of personal and financial disasters.

The ghost of William Larnach is said to haunt the castle to this day, with sightings of his figure in the upper rooms of the castle, particularly in the study where he spent much of his time before his death. Some visitors have reported hearing footsteps and seeing doors open and close by themselves, while others have felt an oppressive atmosphere in certain parts of the castle.

In addition to William Larnach, the spirit of his daughter, Kate, who died at an early age, is also said to haunt the castle. Kate's ghost is often seen in the ballroom, where she loved to dance when she was alive. Guests and staff have reported seeing a woman in a flowing gown dancing alone in the room, her figure vanishing as they approach.

Larnach Castle's haunted reputation is a testament to the tragedies that befell the Larnach family, and the ghosts that are said to inhabit the castle are reminders of the sorrow and loss that once filled its halls. The castle's connection to New Zealand's colonial history, combined with the personal tragedies of the Larnach family, make it one of the country's most haunted locations.

Conclusion of Chapter 5

The ghost stories of Oceania reflect the region's unique blend of indigenous spiritual beliefs and colonial history. In Australia, the spirits of convicts, settlers, and tragic figures linger in the places where they suffered, while in New Zealand, the wairua of the Māori people continue to protect and watch over the land and its people. These ghostly tales are more than just stories of fear—they are reflections of the cultural and historical forces that have shaped the region.

As you explore the haunted places of Oceania, you will encounter spirits that serve as guardians of the past, protectors of sacred lands, and reminders of the suffering and loss that have marked these islands. The ghost stories of Oceania are deeply tied to the land itself, where the physical and spiritual worlds are often seen as inseparable, and where the spirits of the dead remain close to the living.

Chapter 6:

Ghosts of the Middle East

The Middle East, often referred to as the cradle of civilization, is a region steeped in history, with ancient cities, holy lands, and cultural crossroads that date back thousands of years. The ghost stories of the Middle East are deeply influenced by the region's religious and spiritual beliefs, particularly Islam, Judaism, and early regional mythologies. Unlike traditional Western ghost stories, which often revolve around restless spirits or haunted houses, many Middle

Eastern ghost stories center on jinn, otherworldly beings capable of influencing the human world.

In this chapter, we explore the ghost stories and supernatural beings that have captivated the imagination of the Middle East for centuries, focusing on the powerful spirits known as jinn, haunted ruins, and cursed locations that reflect the region's complex spiritual landscape.

Jinn: The Supernatural Beings of Islamic Tradition

In Islamic belief, jinn are supernatural beings created by God from smokeless fire, distinct from humans (who are made of clay) and angels (who are made of light). Jinn are mentioned in the Quran, and they are a race of sentient beings who, like humans, possess free will and can choose between good and evil. Some jinn are benevolent, while others are malevolent, often causing harm or mischief in the human world.

The stories of jinn in Middle Eastern folklore are numerous, and their presence is often invoked to explain mysterious or unexplainable events. Jinn are believed to inhabit remote or desolate places, such as ruins, caves, and deserts, and they are often blamed for hauntings, possessions, and bad luck.

The Jinn of Al-Jazirah Al-Hamra

One of the most famous haunted locations in the Middle East is **Al-Jazirah Al-Hamra**, a deserted village located in the United Arab Emirates. Once a thriving pearl-diving town, the village was abandoned in the 1960s, and since then, it has gained a reputation for being haunted by jinn. Al-Jazirah Al-Hamra's crumbling buildings, empty streets, and eerie atmosphere have made it a popular destination for ghost hunters and paranormal enthusiasts.

Visitors to the abandoned village have reported strange occurrences, such as hearing disembodied voices, footsteps, and even sightings of shadowy figures moving through the ruins. Some claim to have seen lights flickering in the empty homes or heard the sound of children laughing, even though the village has been abandoned for decades.

The belief that Al-Jazirah Al-Hamra is haunted by jinn is deeply rooted in local folklore. According to tradition, jinn are known to inhabit abandoned places, and those who disturb these locations risk incurring their wrath. The jinn of Al-Jazirah Al-Hamra are said to be particularly vengeful, and stories of people being chased or frightened away by these spirits are common.

The haunting of Al-Jazirah Al-Hamra reflects the ancient belief in jinn as powerful and unpredictable beings who inhabit the edges of the human world. The fear of jinn is a significant aspect of Middle Eastern spiritual life, with many taking precautions to avoid attracting their attention, particularly in isolated or deserted places.

The Possession by Jinn

One of the most common ways that jinn interact with humans in Middle Eastern folklore is through possession. It is believed that jinn, especially those who are malevolent, can take control of a person's body and mind, causing them to act erratically or fall ill. Islamic exorcism, known as *ruqyah*, is often used to drive out these spirits, and the process involves the recitation of verses from the Quran and specific prayers meant to expel the jinn.

In traditional stories, jinn possession can occur for several reasons. Sometimes, it is the result of a curse, or a hex placed by someone who has invoked the jinn, while in other cases, it may happen when a person accidentally disturbs a jinn's dwelling. For example, in some regions, it is believed that urinating on certain stones or trees can anger a jinn, leading to possession or other forms of retribution.

The belief in jinn possession is still prevalent in many parts of the Middle East today. While modern medicine is often sought for physical ailments, cases of spiritual or psychological distress are sometimes attributed to jinn, and traditional healers are called upon to perform exorcisms. Stories of jinn possession are particularly common in rural areas, where the connection to ancient traditions and beliefs remains strong.

Haunted Palaces and Cursed Sites

The Middle East is home to some of the world's oldest cities, many of which have witnessed war, conquest, and disaster. Over the centuries, numerous palaces, temples, and ruins have gained a reputation for being haunted by the spirits of those who died violent or untimely deaths. Some of these sites are also said to be cursed, with misfortune befalling those who disturb them.

The Haunted Ruins of Palmyra

Palmyra, an ancient city located in modern-day Syria, is one of the most famous archaeological sites in the world. Once a bustling trade center and cultural crossroads, Palmyra's ruins now stand as a testament to its rich history and tragic fate. The city was destroyed multiple times throughout its history, most recently during the Syrian civil war, when its ancient monuments were severely damaged by militants.

Local folklore tells of ghostly apparitions that haunt the ruins of Palmyra, particularly after sunset. Visitors have reported seeing shadowy figures moving among the columns and hearing the faint sound of voices speaking in ancient tongues. Some believe that the spirits of Palmyra's former inhabitants still linger, trapped in the city they once called home.

The haunting of Palmyra is not just a reflection of its violent past but also of the deep connection between the people and the land. For centuries, Palmyra was a symbol of resilience and beauty, and the spirits that are said to wander its ruins are a reminder of the city's enduring legacy.

The Cursed Treasury of Petra

The ancient city of Petra in Jordan, known for its stunning rock-cut architecture, has long been associated with mystery and legend. One of the most famous stories about Petra involves the *Al-Khazneh* or "The Treasury," a magnificent tomb carved into the cliffs. According to local legend, the Treasury was once home to a vast fortune, hidden by a powerful pharaoh. However, the treasure is said to be cursed, and anyone who tries to claim it will be met with death.

Over the years, many have attempted to find the treasure of Petra, but all have failed. Some claim that the spirits of those who died in the search for the treasure haunt the site, their restless souls guarding the wealth they could never obtain. Visitors to Petra have reported hearing strange noises near the Treasury, and some have even claimed to see ghostly figures watching from the shadows.

The curse of Petra's Treasury reflects the Middle Eastern tradition of cautionary tales, where greed and hubris are often punished by the supernatural. The spirits that are said to haunt the site serve as warnings to those who seek to disturb the ancient secrets of the past.

Egypt – The Pharaohs' Curse and Haunted Tombs

Egypt is home to some of the world's most famous ancient monuments, including the pyramids of Giza and the Valley of the Kings. The ghost stories and legends that surround these sites are deeply tied to the ancient Egyptian belief in the afterlife, where the dead were thought to journey to the underworld, protected by magical spells and sacred objects.

One of the most enduring ghost stories from Egypt is that of the **Pharaohs' Curse**, a tale that has captured the imagination of people around the world for more than a century.

The Curse of Tutankhamun

In 1922, British archaeologist Howard Carter discovered the tomb of the young Pharaoh Tutankhamun in the Valley of the Kings. The discovery was hailed as one of the most significant archaeological finds of all time, but it soon became associated with tragedy. Following the opening of the tomb, several members of Carter's team, as well as others who had been involved in the excavation, died under mysterious circumstances. The press quickly attributed these deaths to the "Curse of the Pharaohs," claiming that Tutankhamun's spirit was seeking revenge for the disturbance of his final resting place.

The idea of the Pharaohs' Curse spread rapidly, with sensational stories of strange illnesses, accidents, and unexplained deaths befalling those who had entered the tomb. Lord Carnarvon, who financed the expedition, died of an infected mosquito bite shortly after the tomb was opened, further fuelling speculation about the curse.

While modern historians and scientists have dismissed the curse as mere coincidence, the story continues to captivate people worldwide. The Curse of Tutankhamun has become a central part of Egypt's haunted legacy, and many still believe that disturbing the tombs of the pharaohs can bring misfortune.

The Ghosts of the Pyramids

The Great Pyramids of Giza, one of the Seven Wonders of the Ancient World, have long been associated with supernatural phenomena. Local guides and workers in the area often speak of strange occurrences near the pyramids at night, including unexplained lights, voices, and figures that appear to vanish upon approach.

One of the most persistent legends involves the ghost of Pharaoh Khufu, the ruler who commissioned the Great Pyramid. It is said that his spirit still watches over the pyramid, ensuring that his tomb remains undisturbed. Some visitors have claimed to see a figure dressed in ancient royal garments near the pyramid, only for it to disappear moments later.

The pyramids are not just monumental tombs; they are symbols of ancient power and the belief in eternal life. The ghost stories that surround them reflect the awe and mystery that these structures continue to inspire, as well as the enduring connection between the living and the dead in Egyptian culture.

Conclusion of Chapter 6

The ghost stories of the Middle East are deeply intertwined with the region's spiritual and religious beliefs. From the mischievous and powerful jinn to the spirits of ancient cities like Palmyra and Petra, these tales reflect the region's complex relationship with the supernatural. Ghosts in Middle Eastern folklore is often seen as both protectors and punishers, enforcing moral lessons, and reminding the living of the consequences of greed, pride, and disrespect for the dead.

As you explore the haunted ruins, cursed treasures, and possessed souls of the Middle East, you will discover that the spirits of the past are not just remnants of history—they are active participants in the ongoing spiritual life of the region. The ghost stories of the Middle East remind us that the boundary between the physical and spiritual worlds is often thin, and that the dead continue to influence the world of the living in profound and mysterious ways.

Chapter 7:

Ghosts of Northern Europe

The vast, cold landscapes of Scandinavia and Northern Europe, with their snow-covered forests, deep fjords, and long, dark winters, have inspired ghost stories and supernatural legends for centuries. In these regions, the line between the natural world and the supernatural has always been thin, with spirits and creatures often said to roam the wild places and abandoned settlements. The haunting beauty of Northern Europe's landscapes, combined with its ancient Viking traditions, Norse mythology, and medieval history, have given rise to some of the most chilling ghost stories in the world.

In this chapter, we explore the ghost stories of Norway, Sweden, Finland, and Iceland, as well as other Northern European countries, focusing on haunted castles, mysterious figures, and the restless spirits that wander these frozen lands.

Norway – The Draugr and Haunted Fjords

Norway, with its majestic fjords and rugged coastline, is a land deeply connected to its Viking past. The Viking age, which lasted from the 8th to the 11th centuries, left behind a rich legacy of mythology, including tales of warriors, gods, and the undead. One of the most famous supernatural beings in Norwegian folklore is the **Draugr**, an undead creature that roams the earth seeking revenge or guarding treasure.

The Draugr: Guardians of the Dead

In Norse mythology, the **Draugr** is a reanimated corpse, often a warrior who was buried with great wealth or power. Unlike traditional ghosts, which are often seen as ethereal and non-corporeal, the Draugr is a physical being, often described as grotesque and decayed, with superhuman strength and the ability to shape-shift. It is said that the Draugr can pass through walls, control the weather, and even cause madness in those who encounter it.

One of the most famous stories of the Draugr comes from the Icelandic sagas, where these creatures are described as the restless dead who rise from their graves to haunt the living. In Norwegian folklore, the Draugr is often associated with ancient burial mounds, where warriors and chieftains were buried with their weapons and treasures. Those who disturb these graves risk invoking the wrath of the Draugr, who will stop at nothing to protect what is theirs.

The Draugr's connection to the Viking age reflects the ancient belief in the power of the dead and the fear that those who died violently or with unresolved grudges could return to wreak havoc on the living. In many stories, the only way to stop a Draugr is to decapitate it or burn its body, ensuring that it can no longer rise from the grave.

In modern Norway, the legend of the Draugr lives on, particularly in rural areas where ancient burial sites are still visible. Visitors to the fjords and remote villages often hear stories of mysterious figures seen at night, standing watch over the ancient mounds, and strange occurrences attributed to the restless spirits of the Viking age.

The Haunting of Akershus Fortress

Akershus Fortress, located in Oslo, is one of Norway's most famous haunted locations. Built in the late 13th century, the fortress has served as a royal residence, a military stronghold, and a prison. Over the centuries, it has been the site of numerous executions, battles, and imprisonments, and it is said that the spirits of those who died within its walls still haunt the fortress to this day.

One of the most famous ghosts of Akershus Fortress is that of a woman known as "Mannen uten Hode," or "The Headless Woman." According to legend, she was a servant who was beheaded for a crime she did not commit. Her headless figure has been seen wandering the halls of the fortress, particularly near the dungeons where prisoners were once held. Witnesses have reported feeling a sudden chill in the air before seeing her ghostly figure, often accompanied by the faint sound of footsteps.

In addition to the Headless Woman, Akershus Fortress is said to be haunted by the spirit of a demon dog known as **Malcanisen**. Legend has it that Malcanisen was once a guard dog that patrolled the fortress grounds, and after its death, it returned as a spectral creature. The ghostly dog is said to appear before significant events or tragedies, serving as an omen of death. Those who see the dog are believed to be cursed, often falling ill, or dying soon after.

Akershus Fortress's haunted history is a reflection of Norway's long and often bloody past, with the spirits of those who suffered within its walls continuing to haunt the living. The fortress's connection to Norway's medieval and wartime history makes it one of the most intriguing, haunted sites in Scandinavia.

Sweden - The Grey Lady and Other Royal Ghosts

Sweden, like its Scandinavian neighbours, has a rich history of ghost stories, many of which are tied to its royal past. Castles, palaces, and manor houses across Sweden are said to be haunted by the spirits of kings, queens, and nobles, many of whom met tragic ends.

The Grey Lady of Drottningholm Palace

One of the most famous ghost stories in Sweden is that of the **Grey Lady**, a spectral figure who is said to haunt **Drottningholm Palace**, the official residence of the Swedish royal family. The palace, located on the island of Lovön in Lake Mälaren, dates to the late 16th century and has been the site of many major events in Swedish history.

The Grey Lady is believed to be the ghost of a former nursemaid or servant who worked at the palace. According to legend, she was deeply devoted to the royal family, and after her death, her spirit remained at the palace, continuing to watch over its inhabitants. The Grey Lady is often seen wearing a long grey dress, moving silently through the palace's corridors, and appearing to visitors and staff.

Those who encounter the Grey Lady often report a sense of calm, as though she is a protective presence rather than a malevolent spirit. However, her sudden appearances can still be unsettling, and she is said to be most active at night, particularly in the older sections of the palace.

The Grey Lady's story is just one of many royal ghost tales in Sweden, where the country's long history of monarchy and nobility has left behind a legacy of haunted palaces and castles.

The Phantom of Stockholm's Royal Palace

Another famous haunting in Sweden is that of **Stockholm's Royal Palace**, the official residence of the Swedish monarchy. Built in the Baroque style in the 18th century, the palace has been the site of numerous royal events, and it is said to be haunted by several ghosts, including that of King Charles XII.

Charles XII, one of Sweden's most famous warrior kings, died in battle in 1718 under mysterious circumstances. Some claim that he was assassinated, while others believe he was killed by a stray bullet. His ghost is said to haunt the palace, particularly in the rooms where he once resided. Visitors and staff have reported hearing footsteps and seeing a shadowy figure dressed in military attire, believed to be the restless spirit of the king.

In addition to Charles XII, the palace is also said to be haunted by a spectral figure known as the "White Lady." This ghost is believed to be a harbinger of death, appearing before the passing of a member of the royal family. The White Lady is often seen wearing a long white dress, her face hidden by a veil. Her appearances are rare but always cause great concern among the palace staff, as they are seen as a warning of impending tragedy.

The ghosts of Stockholm's Royal Palace reflect the long and often turbulent history of Sweden's monarchy, where political intrigue, assassination, and betrayal were common. The spirits that are said to linger in the palace are reminders of the country's royal past and the personal tragedies that often-accompanied life at court.

Finland – The Spirits of Abandoned Villages

Finland's ghost stories are deeply connected to its natural landscape, particularly the forests, lakes, and remote villages that define the country's geography. The Finnish people have long believed in the presence of spirits, both good and evil, that inhabit the natural world, and many of the country's ghost stories reflect this close connection to nature.

The Haunting of Ruinousjärvi Village

One of the most famous haunted locations in Finland is the abandoned village of **Ruinousjärvi**, located in the northern part of the country. Once a thriving farming community, the village was abandoned in the early 20th century due to harsh winters and difficult living conditions. Today, the village's empty houses and overgrown fields create an eerie atmosphere, and it is said that the spirits of the former inhabitants still linger in the area.

Visitors to Ruinousjärvi have reported hearing strange noises, such as the sound of horses' hooves on the old roads or the faint murmur of voices in the empty houses. Some claim to have seen figures dressed in old-fashioned clothing, walking through the fields, or standing at the windows of the abandoned homes.

These figures often disappear upon approach, leaving behind only the unsettling sense that the village is not as empty as it seems.

The haunting of Ruinousjärvi reflects Finland's rural past, where isolation and hardship were common, and many villages were eventually abandoned as people moved to more prosperous areas. The spirits that are said to haunt the village serve as reminders of the lives that were once lived there and the challenges faced by those who tried to make a home in the unforgiving landscape.

The Ghosts of Suomenlinna Fortress

Suomenlinna, a sea fortress located off the coast of Helsinki, is one of Finland's most famous historical sites. Built in the 18th century by the Swedish as a defence against Russian expansion, the fortress has a long and complex history, including battles, occupations, and even a period as a prison camp during the Finnish Civil War.

The fortress is said to be haunted by the spirits of soldiers who died in battle, as well as prisoners who perished during their time at the camp. Visitors to Suomenlinna have reported hearing gunfire and cannon blasts, even though the fortress has been quiet for over a century. Others have seen ghostly figures in military uniforms walking along the walls or standing guard at the entrances to the old bunkers.

One of the most famous spirits associated with Suomenlinna is that of a young soldier who died in a tragic accident. According to legend, the soldier was killed when one of the cannons misfired, and his ghost has been seen patrolling the fortress grounds ever since. Those who encounter the soldier's spirit often report a feeling of sadness, as though the ghost is still mourning his sudden death.

The ghosts of Suomenlinna reflect Finland's long history of conflict and occupation, with the spirits of soldiers and prisoners serving as reminders of the fortress's role in the country's defence and struggle for independence.

Iceland - The Hidden People and Haunted Waterfalls

Iceland's ghost stories are deeply influenced by the country's unique landscape and its ancient beliefs in the *huldufólk* or "hidden people." The hidden people are said to be supernatural beings who live in the rocks, mountains, and waterfalls of Iceland, and they are often seen as protectors of the land. However, they can also be vengeful if disturbed, leading to many stories of hauntings and strange occurrences.

The Haunting of Skógafoss Waterfall

One of the most famous haunted locations in Iceland is **Skógafoss**, a stunning waterfall located in the southern part of the country. According to legend, a treasure chest was hidden behind the waterfall by one of the country's early Viking settlers, and the spirit of the Viking still guards the treasure to this day. Visitors to the waterfall have reported seeing a ghostly figure standing near the base of the falls, often accompanied by the sound of chains rattling.

In addition to the Viking spirit, Skógafoss is also said to be home to the hidden people, who are believed to live in the rocks and cliffs surrounding the waterfall. Those who disturb the hidden people by moving rocks or building too close to their homes are said to experience misfortune, including illness, accidents, and even death. The hidden people are often seen as protectors of Iceland's natural landscape, ensuring that the land remains undisturbed by human activity.

The haunting of Skógafoss reflects Iceland's deep connection to its Viking past and its belief in the supernatural beings that inhabit the land. The spirits that are said to haunt the waterfall serve as both protectors and warnings, reminding visitors of the ancient traditions and beliefs that still shape the country's culture.

Conclusion of Chapter 7

The ghost stories of Northern Europe are as wild and untamed as the landscapes they inhabit. From the undead Draugr of Norway's fjords to the Grey Lady of Sweden's royal palaces, these tales reflect the region's deep connection to its Viking past, medieval history, and ancient folklore. The spirits that haunt these frozen lands are not just figures of fear; they are guardians of the past, protectors of sacred places, and reminders of the fragility of life in a harsh and unforgiving environment.

As you journey through the haunted castles, abandoned villages, and misty fjords of Northern Europe, you will encounter ghosts that are as ancient as the land itself. These spirits, whether seeking revenge, guarding treasure, or simply watching over the living, that the past is never truly gone—it lingers in the stories we tell and the places we call home.

Chapter 8:

Ghosts of Eastern Europe and Russia

Eastern Europe and Russia are lands of deep forests, ancient cities, and long, harsh winters. Throughout their turbulent histories, filled with war, conquest, and political upheaval, these regions have developed a rich tradition of ghost stories that are as dark and mysterious as the landscapes themselves. From the vengeful spirits of Russian royalty to the haunted castles of Hungary, the ghost stories of Eastern Europe and Russia reflect the cultural and historical complexities of these regions.

In this chapter, we will explore some of the most famous and spine-chilling ghost stories from countries such as Russia, Poland, Hungary, and Romania, delving into haunted palaces, eerie castles, and supernatural beings from Slavic folklore.

Russia – The Ghosts of the Romanovs and the Restless Spirits of Moscow

Russia's long and often tragic history has given rise to numerous ghost stories, many of which are tied to the country's royal family, the Romanovs, as well as its dark political past. Ghosts in Russian folklore is often seen as vengeful or tragic figures, reflecting the suffering and violence that have marked the country's history.

The Ghosts of the Romanov Family

One of the most famous ghost stories in Russia revolves around the tragic fate of the Romanov family, the last royal family of Russia. In 1917, during the Russian Revolution, Tsar Nicholas II, his wife Alexandra, and their five children were forced to abdicate the throne and were eventually imprisoned by the Bolsheviks. In 1918, the entire family was executed in a basement in Yekaterinburg, a violent end to centuries of royal rule in Russia.

Since their deaths, numerous reports have emerged of sightings of the Romanov family's ghosts. In particular, the ghost of Grand Duchess Anastasia, the youngest daughter, has been seen wandering the halls of old royal palaces, dressed in the clothes she wore during her imprisonment. Many have claimed that she appears as a sorrowful figure, as though seeking justice for the terrible fate that befell her family.

The execution site in Yekaterinburg is now marked by a church, and visitors to the site have reported strange occurrences, such as hearing whispers, footsteps, and the sound of a woman weeping. The Romanov family's tragic story and the mystery surrounding their deaths have contributed to their haunting legacy, and their spirits are said to linger in the places where they lived and died.

The haunting of the Romanovs reflects the deep scars left by the Russian Revolution and the subsequent fall of the Russian Empire. The spirits of the royal family are seen not just as ghostly figures, but as symbols of a lost era, forever wandering the world they once ruled.

The Kremlin Ghosts: Restless Spirits of Political Power

The **Kremlin**, the heart of Russian political power in Moscow, is not only one of the most historically significant locations in Russia but also one of the most haunted. Over the centuries, the Kremlin has witnessed countless events of political intrigue, assassination, and betrayal, and it is said that the ghosts of those who died within its walls still linger.

One of the most famous ghosts of the Kremlin is that of **Ivan the Terrible**, Russia's first tsar, who ruled in the 16th century. Ivan was known for his brutal reign, marked by violence, paranoia, and executions. According to legend, Ivan's ghost has been seen in the Kremlin's Ivan the Great Bell Tower, where he is said to appear on the eve of significant political events or tragedies. His spirit is described as tall and imposing, dressed in the traditional garb of a tsar, and those who see him often report feeling a sense of dread.

Another ghost associated with the Kremlin is that of **Catherine the Great**, one of Russia's most powerful and influential rulers. Catherine's ghost is said to haunt the Kremlin Palace, where she lived during her reign. Visitors have reported seeing her spirit in the hallways, and some claim to hear the sound of her footsteps echoing through the palace late at night.

In addition to Ivan the Terrible and Catherine the Great, the Kremlin is also said to be haunted by the ghosts of political figures from more recent history. One of the most notorious figures is **Joseph Stalin**, whose spirit has been reportedly seen in the Kremlin, often appearing near the offices where he once worked. The sight of Stalin's ghost is said to be accompanied by a chilling cold and a sense of unease, a reflection of the fear and repression that marked his reign.

The ghost stories of the Kremlin reflect the complex relationship between power, history, and death in Russia. The spirits that haunt its walls serve as reminders of the brutal and often tragic events that have shaped the country's past.

Poland – The Wawel Dragon and Haunted Castles

Poland's ghost stories are deeply tied to its medieval past, with many of the country's haunted locations dating back to the time of kings, knights, and castles. These stories often involve vengeful spirits, cursed lands, and supernatural creatures that have long been part of Polish folklore.

The Wawel Dragon: A Creature of Legend

One of the most famous legends in Poland is that of the **Wawel Dragon**, a mythical creature that is said to have once lived in a cave beneath **Wawel Castle** in Kraków. According to legend, the dragon terrorized the people of Kraków, devouring livestock and even villagers. The king promised the hand of his daughter to anyone who could slay the dragon, and after many failed attempts, a clever cobbler finally managed to defeat the beast by feeding it a sheep stuffed with sulphur. The dragon drank from the Vistula River to quench its thirst and exploded, freeing the city from its reign of terror.

While the Wawel Dragon is a creature of legend, the cave beneath the castle, known as **Smocza Jama** (Dragon's Den), is said to be haunted by the spirit of the dragon. Visitors to the cave have reported hearing strange noises, feeling sudden drops in temperature, and even seeing a shadowy figure resembling a dragon's outline. Some believe that the dragon's spirit still guards the cave, protecting the treasures said to be hidden within.

The story of the Wawel Dragon is one of Poland's most enduring legends, blending folklore with the country's medieval history. The dragon's spirit, whether real or imagined, serves as a reminder of the ancient myths that continue to shape the cultural landscape of Poland.

The Haunted Castles of Poland

Poland is home to numerous haunted castles, many of which have dark histories filled with betrayal, murder, and political intrigue. One of the most famous haunted locations in Poland is **Ogrodzieniec Castle**, a medieval fortress located in the Silesian region. The castle, which dates to the 14th century, was the site of many battles and sieges, and its ruins are now said to be haunted by the spirits of those who died within its walls.

One of the most famous spirits associated with Ogrodzieniec Castle is that of **Stanislaw Warszycki**, a notorious noble person who was known for his cruelty and ruthlessness. After his death, Warszycki's ghost is said to have returned to the castle, often appearing as a black dog with glowing red eyes. The dog is believed to be a manifestation of Warszycki's spirit, cursed to guard the castle for eternity as punishment for his wicked deeds.

Visitors to Ogrodzieniec Castle have reported seeing shadowy figures, hearing ghostly voices, and feeling an overwhelming sense of fear in certain areas of the ruins. The haunting of Ogrodzieniec reflects Poland's medieval history, where political power and personal ambition often led to violence and betrayal, leaving behind spirits that are forever tied to the places where they met their tragic ends.

Hungary – The Cursed Castle of Csejte and the Bloody Countess

Hungary's ghost stories are filled with tales of cursed castles, vengeful spirits, and dark legends that reflect the country's medieval past. One of the most infamous figures in Hungarian history is **Elizabeth Báthory**, a noble person who became known as the "Blood Countess" for her alleged crimes against young girls. Her story, combined with the haunted legacy of her castle, has made her one of the most notorious figures in European ghost lore.

The Haunting of Csejte Castle

Csejte Castle, located in present-day Slovakia but historically part of the Kingdom of Hungary, was the home of **Elizabeth Báthory**, a countess who lived in the late 16th and early 17th centuries. Báthory became infamous for allegedly torturing and killing hundreds of young girls, many of whom were servants or peasant girls from the surrounding villages. According to legend, Báthory believed that bathing in the blood of virgins would preserve her youth, and she carried out these horrific acts in secret for many years.

After her crimes were discovered, Báthory was arrested and imprisoned in her castle, where she spent the last years of her life in isolation. She died in 1614, but her dark legacy lives on, and her spirit is said to haunt Csejte Castle to this day.

Visitors to the castle have reported hearing the screams of young girls, as well as seeing the ghostly figure of Báthory herself, often described as a pale woman in a blood-stained gown. Some claim to have felt a cold, oppressive presence in the castle's dungeons, where Báthory is believed to have carried out her gruesome deeds.

The story of Elizabeth Báthory has become a legend in Hungary and beyond, blending historical fact with dark folklore. The haunting of Csejte Castle reflects the fear and fascination with the macabre that has surrounded Báthory's story for centuries, making her one of the most notorious figures in European ghost lore.

Romania – The Ghosts of Transylvania and Vlad the Impaler

When it comes to ghost stories, few places in the world are as famous as **Transylvania**, the region in Romania that has become synonymous with vampires and the supernatural. Transylvania's dark forests, medieval castles, and towering Carpathian Mountains create the perfect setting for tales of haunted places and mysterious creatures. While the region's most famous figure is **Vlad the Impaler**, the inspiration for Bram Stoker's *Dracula*, Transylvania is also home to numerous ghost stories and haunted locations.

Bran Castle: Dracula's Alleged Lair

Bran Castle, often referred to as "Dracula's Castle," is one of Romania's most visited tourist destinations, due to its association with the legendary vampire. While there is no historical evidence that Vlad the Impaler, the real-life inspiration for Dracula, ever lived in the castle, Bran Castle has become a symbol of Transylvania's dark and mysterious past.

The castle, which dates to the 14th century, is said to be haunted by the spirits of those who died within its walls, including prisoners and soldiers from various battles. Visitors have reported hearing strange noises, such as footsteps and whispers, as well as seeing ghostly figures moving through the castle's shadowy corridors. Some claim to have seen the figure of a man dressed in a black cloak, believed to be the ghost of Vlad the Impaler himself.

In addition to the legend of Dracula, Bran Castle is also said to be haunted by the spirits of its former residents, including Queen Marie of Romania, who lived in the castle during the early 20th century. Queen Marie's ghost is often described as a peaceful presence, watching over the castle that she loved during her lifetime.

The ghost stories of Bran Castle reflect Romania's long and complex history, where myth and reality often intertwine. The association with Dracula has only added to the castle's haunted reputation, making it one of the most famous haunted locations in the world.

The Haunted Forest of Hoia Baciu

Just outside the city of Cluj-Napoca in Transylvania lies the **Hoia Baciu Forest**, often referred to as "the most haunted forest in the world." The forest has gained a reputation for being a place of supernatural occurrences, including ghost sightings, mysterious lights, and even UFO activity. Locals avoid the forest, believing that it is cursed or inhabited by malevolent spirits.

One of the most common reports from those who enter the forest is the feeling of being watched, as well as hearing disembodied voices and seeing shadowy figures among the trees. Some have claimed to experience sudden nausea, dizziness, or even the sensation of time loss after spending time in the forest.

The Hoia Baciu Forest's reputation as a haunted and mysterious place has drawn paranormal investigators and thrill-seekers from around the world, all hoping to catch a glimpse of the supernatural forces said to inhabit the area. The forest's eerie atmosphere and unexplained phenomena have made it a focal point of Romania's ghost lore, adding to the country's already rich tradition of supernatural stories.

Conclusion of Chapter 8

The ghost stories of Eastern Europe and Russia are steeped in the region's long and often violent history. From the restless spirits of Russian royalty to the cursed castles of Hungary, these tales reflect the tragedies and mysteries of the past. The spirits that haunt these lands serve as reminders of the political intrigue, betrayal, and suffering that have shaped the region's history for centuries.

As you explore the haunted palaces, cursed castles, and dark forests of Eastern Europe and Russia, you will encounter spirits that are as complex and enigmatic as the lands they inhabit. These ghost stories are more than just tales of fear—they are reflections of the cultural, historical, and spiritual forces that continue to shape the region to this day.

Chapter G:

Ghosts of South Asia

South Asia, with its diverse cultures, ancient religions, and storied past, is a land filled with spiritual richness and ghostly tales. Ghost stories in this region are often deeply intertwined with local beliefs in reincarnation, karma, and the supernatural, blending Hindu, Muslim, Buddhist, and folk traditions. The spirits of the dead are seen as both benevolent protectors and vengeful forces, depending on how they were treated in life and in death.

In this chapter, we delve into the eerie and spine-chilling ghost stories from South Asia, exploring the haunted palaces of India, the restless spirits of Pakistan, the jinn of Bangladesh, and the terrifying creatures of Sri Lanka's folklore.

India – The Churails and Haunted Palaces

India is a land of ancient traditions, spirituality, and mysticism, where the belief in ghosts and spirits is deeply ingrained in the culture. Indian ghost stories often revolve around concepts of karma, unfinished business, and the eternal cycle of life, death, and rebirth. Many of these stories involve spirits that seek justice, revenge, or release from their earthly ties.

The Churail: India's Most Feared Female Spirit

One of the most feared supernatural beings in Indian folklore is the **Churail**, a vengeful female spirit who preys on men, especially those who have wronged women during their lifetimes. The Churail is believed to be the ghost of a woman who died during childbirth or was mistreated by her family, and her spirit returns to exact revenge on those who caused her suffering.

Churails are often depicted as grotesque figures with backward-facing feet, a sign that they are no longer bound by the laws of the living world. In some stories, they can transform into beautiful women to lure men into traps before revealing their true, terrifying form. Once the Churail captures her victim, she drains his life force, leaving him a lifeless shell.

Churail stories are common in rural parts of India, particularly in the northern states, where belief in spirits and the supernatural remains strong. Many villages still observe rituals to ward off Churails, including the use of talismans and prayers to protect men from these vengeful spirits.

One famous story of the Churail comes from the state of Rajasthan, where a wealthy noble person wronged his wife by abandoning her for another woman. After her death, his wife returned as a Churail, haunting the nobleman's estate, and slowly draining the life force of every man in the household. The legend claims that her ghost still haunts the region, seeking vengeance on those who mistreat women.

The Churail is more than just a ghost story; she is a powerful symbol of female anger and retribution, reflecting the deep gender dynamics in Indian society. The stories of Churails serve as cautionary tales, warning men to treat women with respect and dignity or face the consequences.

The Haunted Palace of Bhangarh

India is also home to some of the world's most famously haunted locations, including **Bhangarh Fort**, a 17th-century fortress located in the state of Rajasthan. Bhangarh Fort is often considered one of the most haunted places in India, with numerous legends surrounding its mysterious abandonment and the spirits said to roam its ruins.

According to local legend, a powerful sorcerer fell in love with the princess of Bhangarh and tried to use magic to make her fall in love with him. However, the princess saw through his trickery and rejected his advances. Enraged, the sorcerer cursed the entire city, dooming it to destruction. Shortly afterward, Bhangarh was attacked by invaders, and the entire population was slaughtered.

The ruins of Bhangarh Fort are said to be haunted by the spirits of those who died in the attack, and visitors to the fort have reported hearing strange noises, seen ghostly apparitions, and felt an overwhelming sense of dread. The Indian government has even placed signs at the entrance to the fort, warning visitors not to enter after sunset, as it is believed that the spirits are most active at night.

Bhangarh Fort's haunted reputation reflects India's deep connection to its historical past, where curses, magic, and the supernatural are intertwined with real-world events. The spirits that are said to haunt the fort serve as reminders of the violence and betrayal that marked the city's downfall.

The Ghosts of Shaniwarwada Fort

Another famously haunted location in India is **Shaniwarwada Fort**, a historic fortification located in Pune, Maharashtra. Built in the early 18th century, the fort was once the seat of the powerful Peshwa rulers of the Maratha Empire. However, its history is marked by political intrigue, betrayal, and murder, which have given rise to numerous ghost stories.

The most famous ghost associated with Shaniwarwada Fort is that of a young prince named **Narayanrao**, who was brutally murdered by his own relatives in 1773 as part of a political conspiracy. According to legend, Narayanrao's ghost still haunts the fort, and on full moon nights, his spirit can be heard crying out for help, repeating the words "Kaka mala vachva" (Uncle, save me) in Marathi.

Visitors to the fort have reported hearing these ghostly cries at night, as well as experiencing unexplained cold spots, flickering lights, and sudden feelings of fear. The haunting of Shaniwarwada reflects the brutal power struggles of India's royal history, where political ambition often led to bloodshed and betrayal.

Pakistan – *The Jinn of Karachi and the Restless Spirits of the Subcontinent*

In Pakistan, ghost stories often revolve around the concept of **jinn**, supernatural beings mentioned in the Quran. Jinn, much like in other parts of the Muslim world, are believed to be created from smokeless fire and possess free will, much like humans. They can be good or evil, and they are often blamed for hauntings, possessions, and unexplained phenomena.

The Haunting of the Mohatta Palace

One of the most famous haunted locations in Pakistan is **Mohatta Palace**, a beautiful mansion located in Karachi. Built in the 1920s by a wealthy Hindu businessman, the palace is known for its stunning architecture and lush gardens. However, it is also said to be haunted by the spirits of its former inhabitants.

According to local legend, the palace is home to several ghosts, including that of the businessman's wife, who died under mysterious circumstances. Visitors to the palace have reported seeing her ghost wandering the halls, often dressed in traditional attire. Some claim to have heard strange noises, such as footsteps and the sound of crying, while others have experienced sudden cold spots and feelings of unease.

The haunting of Mohatta Palace reflects Pakistan's colonial past, where the opulence of the elite often masked the tragedies that took place behind closed doors. The spirits that are said to inhabit the palace serve as reminders of the human cost of wealth and power.

The Jinn of the Karachi Graveyards

Karachi, Pakistan's largest city, is home to numerous graveyards, many of which are said to be haunted by jinn. One of the most famous graveyards in the city is the **Chowkandi Tombs**, an ancient burial site located on the outskirts of Karachi. The tombs, which date back to the 15th century, are known for their intricate carvings and unique architecture. However, they are also said to be inhabited by jinn, who guard the graves of the dead.

Visitors to the Chowkandi Tombs have reported seeing strange lights, hearing disembodied voices, and feeling an overwhelming sense of dread when walking among the tombs at night. Some claim that the jinn are protective spirits, guarding the tombs from those who would disturb them, while others believe that the jinn are malevolent beings, seeking to harm anyone who enters their domain.

The belief in jinn is deeply rooted in Pakistan's Islamic traditions, and ghost stories involving jinn often serve as cautionary tales, warning people to respect the dead and the supernatural forces that protect them. The haunted graveyards of Karachi reflect the region's complex spiritual landscape, where the boundaries between the living and the dead are often blurred.

Bangladesh – The Ghosts of the Sundarbans and Haunted Mansions

In Bangladesh, ghost stories are often tied to the country's rich natural landscape, particularly the **Sundarbans**, the largest mangrove forest in the world. The Sundarbans are home to numerous dangerous creatures, including the Bengal tiger, but they are also said to be inhabited by supernatural beings and restless spirits.

The Ghosts of the Sundarbans

The Sundarbans have long been considered a place of mystery and danger, with many local legends involving supernatural creatures that haunt the dense forests. One of the most famous ghost stories from the Sundarbans involves the **Bonbibi**, a forest goddess who is said to protect the people of the Sundarbans from evil spirits and wild animals.

According to local tradition, the Sundarbans are inhabited by malevolent spirits known as **Dakkhin Rai**, who take the form of tigers and prey on humans. The Bonbibi is believed to keep these spirits at bay, protecting the people who live and work in the forest. However, those who enter the forest without paying proper respect to the Bonbibi are said to be at risk of falling victim to the vengeful spirits that roam the area.

Many people who venture into the Sundarbans have reported seeing ghostly apparitions, hearing strange noises, and feeling an inexplicable sense of dread. Some claim to have seen figures dressed in white, floating among the trees, while others have encountered the ghostly forms of tigers, their glowing eyes watching from the darkness.

The ghost stories of the Sundarbans reflect the close connection between the people of Bangladesh and their natural environment, where the line between the physical and spiritual worlds is often blurred. The spirits that are said to inhabit the forest serve as both protectors and threats, ensuring that the delicate balance of the ecosystem is maintained.

The Haunted Zamindar Mansions

Bangladesh is also home to numerous **zamindar** mansions, the grand estates of wealthy landowners who ruled over vast tracts of land during the British colonial period. Many of these mansions are now abandoned, their decaying walls and overgrown gardens serving as a reminder of a bygone era. However, they are also said to be haunted by the spirits of their former owners.

One famous haunted mansion is the **Rose Garden Palace** in Dhaka, once the home of a wealthy zamindar. Visitors to the mansion have reported hearing strange noises, such as the sound of furniture moving and footsteps echoing through the empty halls. Some claim to have seen the ghost of the zamindar himself, dressed in traditional clothing, wandering the grounds of the estate.

The haunting of the Rose Garden Palace reflects the decline of the zamindar class in the aftermath of Bangladesh's independence, where the opulence of the colonial period gave way to abandonment and decay. The spirits that are said to haunt the mansion serve as reminders of the social and political changes that have shaped the country's history.

Sri Lanka - The Ghosts of Colonial Ceylon and the Demon of the Hills

Sri Lanka's ghost stories are deeply tied to the island's colonial past, where the influence of the Portuguese, Dutch, and British has left a lasting impact on the culture and folklore of the region. The spirits of colonial settlers, as well as the island's indigenous beliefs in supernatural beings, continue to shape the ghost stories of Sri Lanka.

The Haunting of Galle Face Hotel

One of the most famous haunted locations in Sri Lanka is the **Galle Face Hotel**, a colonial-era hotel located in the capital city of Colombo. Built in 1864, the hotel has hosted numerous famous guests over the years, including British royalty and international celebrities. However, it is also said to be haunted by the spirit of a former guest who died under mysterious circumstances.

According to legend, the ghost of **Lady Doris**, a British woman who stayed at the hotel in the early 20th century, still haunts the halls of the Galle Face Hotel. Lady Doris was found dead in her room, and her death was never fully explained. Visitors to the hotel have reported seeing her ghost, often dressed in white, walking along the corridors or sitting on the balcony, staring out at the sea.

The haunting of Galle Face Hotel reflects Sri Lanka's colonial history, where the opulence of the British Empire often masked the darker aspects of life in colonial Ceylon. The spirit of Lady Doris is seen as a reminder of the untold stories and tragedies that took place during this period.

The Demon of Adam's Peak

Adam's Peak, a sacred mountain in central Sri Lanka, is a place of great spiritual significance for Buddhists, Hindus, and Muslims alike. The mountain is believed to be the site where the Buddha, Shiva, or Adam (depending on the religious tradition) left a footprint at the summit, making it a popular pilgrimage site.

However, Adam's Peak is also said to be haunted by a malevolent spirit known as the **Demon of the Hills**. According to local legend, the demon preys on travellers who attempt to climb the mountain without paying proper respect to the sacred site. Those who disrespect the mountain are said to fall victim to accidents, illnesses, or even disappearances, with many attributing these misfortunes to the demon's wrath.

Pilgrims who climb Adam's Peak often perform rituals and prayers to appease the demon and seek protection during their journey. Despite the mountain's spiritual significance, the belief in the demon serves as a reminder of the dangers that still lurk in the natural world.

Conclusion of Chapter G

The ghost stories of South Asia are as varied and complex as the region's cultural and religious landscape. From the vengeful Churails of India to the protective Bonbibi of the Sundarbans, these tales reflect the close connection between the living and the dead, as well as the spiritual forces that shape the world. The spirits that haunt the palaces, forests, and graveyards of South Asia serve as reminders of the region's rich history, where the supernatural is never far from the everyday.

As you explore the haunted mansions, cursed forests, and restless spirits of South Asia, you will encounter ghosts that are both terrifying and protective, reflecting the complex interplay between the physical and spiritual realms in this ancient land.

Conclusion:

The Universal Haunting

Ghost stories have been told and retold for centuries, across every corner of the globe, transcending cultures, languages, and belief systems. While the specific details of these stories differ—shaped by local histories, religions, and traditions—certain themes remain universal. Whether they come from ancient legends or modern urban tales, ghosts are often seen as manifestations of unresolved trauma, unfinished business, or the consequences of past deeds.

From the vengeful spirits of Japan's *Onryo* to the haunted castles of Europe, the spirits that populate these stories remind us that the past is never truly gone—it lingers in the present, waiting to be acknowledged, feared, or understood. Ghosts are not just remnants of the dead; they are reflections of the living. They represent our fears of death, guilt, the unknown, and the unresolved aspects of our own lives.

In each region, ghost stories serve multiple purposes. They teach moral lessons, preserve cultural histories, and offer ways to deal with grief and loss. In Asia, ghosts often represent honour and familial duty, while in the Americas, they may embody the unresolved violence of colonialism and slavery. In Europe, ghosts frequently arise from the personal or political betrayals that marked the continent's long history of monarchies and wars. Meanwhile, Africa's ghost stories reflect the power of the ancestors and the ever-present connection between the living and the spiritual world.

What is particularly fascinating is how these stories evolve over time. While many ghost stories are rooted in ancient folklore, they continue to adapt, absorbing elements of contemporary life. The rise of modern haunted houses, urban legends, and horror films shows that, no matter how far we advance technologically, our fascination with ghosts remains as strong as ever.

By journeying through the haunted lands of Asia, Europe, the Americas, Africa, and beyond, we have glimpsed how the world's cultures interpret the afterlife and the boundaries between the living and the dead. These stories speak to something timeless within us—a desire to understand what happens after death, to make peace with the unknown, and to confront the fears that lurk just beyond the veil.

But beyond the fear and intrigue, ghost stories offer us something more: a reminder of our shared humanity. Whether we believe in ghosts or not, these stories connect us to the past, to our ancestors, and to each other.

Epilogue: Why We Keep Telling Ghost Stories

Ghost stories are not just tales of horror or entertainment; they are an essential part of the human experience. Across cultures and time periods, they serve as a window into the collective fears and hopes of societies. But why do we continue to tell these stories? Why, in an age of science and rationality, do we still find ourselves drawn to the supernatural?

Part of the answer lies in the mysteries that ghost stories explore. Death remains one of the greatest mysteries of all, and ghost stories offer a way to confront it, to give shape to the unknown. By telling these stories, we attempt to make sense of the things that frighten us most—mortality, loss, betrayal, and the idea that the past can never truly be escaped.

In many ways, ghost stories help us navigate our own emotions. They give voice to our fears, our regrets, and our desires for closure. They allow us to explore grief, anger, and the consequences of unresolved wrongs in a safe and controlled way. Through ghost stories, we symbolically bring the dead back to life, if only for a moment, so that we might learn from them.

But ghost stories are also about survival—how we, the living, endure. They remind us that, despite the chaos and unpredictability of life, we have the power to confront our fears, to seek redemption, and to find peace. The spirits that haunt these tales are not just figures of terror—they are guides, urging us to face the things we would rather avoid.

As long as humans exist, we will continue to tell ghost stories. They are as much a part of our shared cultural heritage as any other form of storytelling. They offer a bridge between the living and the dead, the past and the present, the known and the unknown.

So, the next time you hear a strange noise in the night or feel an unexplained chill in the air, remember: the stories we tell about ghosts are not just about the dead—they are about us, the living. They are stories about what it means to be human.

Dear Reader,
Primarily, I want to extend my heartfelt thanks to you for choosing to read my book. Whether this is your first book of mine, or you have followed my work for a while, your time, attention, and support mean everything to me as an author.
I write with the hope that my stories resonate with readers like you, sparking imagination, inspiring thought, and perhaps offering moments of joy, reflection, or discovery. Writing is a deeply personal

endeavour, but it is the readers who truly bring a story to life. Without your engagement, these words would remain just that—words on a page. Instead, they have now become part of a shared experience, one I hope you have enjoyed.

As a writer, I am always striving to grow and improve, and that is where your feedback comes in. If you found the story captivating, if a particular character spoke to you, or if there was a moment that made you laugh, cry, or think, I would love to hear about it. Your review does not have to be long or detailed—even just a few words or a quick rating can make a significant impact.

Leaving a review is not only helpful to me, but it also helps other readers discover new stories that may be a perfect fit for them. In the ever-growing world of books, a recommendation from a fellow reader can be the most powerful motivator for someone deciding which book to pick up next.

I understand how busy life can get, and I deeply appreciate the time it takes to leave feedback. But know that each review truly makes a difference—it encourages me to keep writing, refining, and telling the stories I hope you will continue to enjoy.

Thank you again for your support, and I look forward to your thoughts and reviews. Your words will continue to shape my journey as an author, and I hope you will stay connected as I create more stories to share with you and readers around the world.

With gratitude,

Ray Roberts

This Link will take you straight to the review page -

https://www.amazon.co.uk/review/create-review?&asin=B0DGTCHVJV

Printed in Great Britain
by Amazon